MYSTERIES
OF
THE
UNIVERSE

Kallisto Gaia Press Inc.
1801 E. 51st Street
Suite 365-246
Austin TX 78723
info@kallistogaiapress.org
(254) 654-7205

Cover Design: Preston H. Burnett
Author photo: Nate Boots

ISBN: 978-1-952224-30-0

MYSTERIES OF THE UNIVERSE

10 stories

Roger Hart

Also by Roger Hart

ERRATICS

TABLE OF CONTENTS

for Gwen

OTHER DIMENSIONS

The Bridge

On December 15, 1967, the Silver Bridge connecting Gallipolis, Ohio, to Point Pleasant, West Virginia, collapsed. Forty-six people died. Two were never found. A woman was seen running from the bridge as cars tumbled in the river behind her.

"Don't do it," my dad said.

I was driving the family pickup, a rusted-out Ford with bald tires and a cracked windshield that had won the "Ugliest Truck" contest at the Junior Gallia County Fair the previous two years. A cold December wind blew across the river.

My mother elbowed me in the ribs. "Go on."

My father leaned against the passenger side door, his finger tracing a jagged crack in the window. He groaned. "It's going to kill me."

My mother, squeezed between my father and me, patted my knee and lifted her chin forward. "Ignore him," she said. "Go on."

His refusal to cross the Silver Bridge annoyed her, and his two-footed driving scared her even when he was sober. That afternoon he'd had more than a few drinks with my Uncle Orville.

"I'm jumping out," he said, reaching for the handle of the passenger-side door.

My mother yanked him back. "You're not jumping out, and we're not driving all the way to Pomeroy, so you can avoid this bridge." She shook her head. "I never," she said.

My father buried his face in his hands. "Dying runs in our family," he mumbled.

The bridge shook and rattled as if it might come apart any second. Then, high above the Ohio River, we stopped. My father twisted in his seat and looked at the suspension cables and checked his door and mine to make sure they were unlocked. We were stuck in traffic while we waited for the light on the Ohio side of the river to turn green.

"Oh," he said, clutching the dash after a particularly hard bump shook the truck.

"Jim!" my mother said. "Enough!"

He opened his mouth, started to say something, and stopped.

"Go on," I said.

The bridge shook again.

He mumbled, but the bangs and clanks prevented me from hearing him. "What?" I asked.

A barge loaded with coal slowly passed beneath us. Red and green Christmas lights draped across Front Street were barely visible through the shroud of coal-stoked brown haze that had settled over the river.

"Dying," he said.

I took my eyes off the car stopped in front of us long enough to glance across the front seat. "Dying? What dying?"

"You know, Charlie," he said. "Dying."

We were on our way home from the funeral of Aunt Bessie, my father's oldest sister, who had died of a cracked skull after getting kicked by a Holstein heifer. My grandfather and my Uncle Lou had died four years earlier in a roof fall in Kittany 3, a Foster coalmine across the river in West Virginia. My cousin Bobby, suffering the final stage of Hodgkin's disease, died sitting in a bowling alley while my aunt and uncle argued who could best pick up a 6-10 split. Uncle Roy was leaning against the potbelly stove in his hunting shack on Big Toe Knob when lightning hit the chimney, ran through Roy, and left a six-foot long melted groove in the linoleum floor. But, as my Aunt Lucy always said, *It wasn't lightning that killed Roy. It was his choking on the plug of Mail Pouch after getting lightning struck.* And my cousin Bruce, perhaps the saddest case of all, was poaching deer one cold January night when he bled to death after trying to unzip his coat while forgetting he held his razor-sharp skinning knife.

My father moaned with each rattle of the suspension cables and clang of the decking as cars and trucks heading into West Virginia passed in the opposite lane. "This bridge," he said.

My mother pressed her hand to her breast, and said *pshaw*, not a word so much as a sound of disapproval. She shook her head slightly to let me know I had nothing to worry about. Other than her deep Baptist convictions, she didn't buy into premonitions, curses, or the supernatural. She called my father's idea that the bridge was going to kill him utter nonsense.

My father claimed he knew things, that he had a gift. He saw omens and signs, had premonitions, tingles in the bones. He said it was like radar, a heads-up, a deja before the vu. Bar fights, lightning strikes, flat tires, exploding barbecue grills, he saw them coming before they came. He'd predicted the Cincinnati Reds would finish the season more than ten games out of first place when his buddies at The Little Brown Jug thought they'd win the pennant, and he once warned my mother the clothesline was going to collapse minutes before Monday's wash hit the ground. He said there was no doubt he had the gift although he sometimes ignored the warning or mistook it for an upset stomach caused by bean-loaded chili or a hot dog gone bad.

He was a cautious man in most matters. He avoided the Silver Bridge, the mines, the crazy heifers, lightning storms, and Mail Pouch. He drove up and down the river, Franklin Furnace, South Point, Portsmouth, Peebles, Ripley, a cigarette hanging from the corner of his mouth, one foot on the gas pedal and one foot on the brake, demonstrating for school custodians how Rose Chemical floor wax could make their basketball courts shine. He called himself a chemical salesman, but he was a storyteller, a man who spun mysteries out of the everyday occurrences around town and conversations overheard at the Smiling Skull Saloon. When he couldn't find a mystery, he invented one.

The light at the end of the bridge turned green, and we began to move forward.

The following afternoon my father sat on our back porch with a case of Rolling Rock and a sales receipt pad from Rose Chemical and stared at the muddy Ohio churning along the bank at the bottom of the hill, the scene blurred by pollution from coal plants and the plastic sheets covering the screen windows. He set his bottle down and wrote a few words in the notebook he held on his lap, his left hand smearing the letters as fast as he wrote them. After filling up one page, he stopped, put the pencil down and went back to looking at the river. "Why'd you stop?" I asked.

"Looking for a happy ending," he said. "They're hard to find."

His feet were on the windowsill, and his toes, poking out of holes in his socks, touched the plastic covering the screens. "Well?" he said, his bloodshot eyes staring at me.

"Well, what?"

"You believe?"

I knew what he was asking. It wasn't a religious question, one that my mother or Reverend Emerick might ask, but a question of whether I believed my father had a gift, or curse, for occasionally seeing the future. My passion was science. Apollo 4 had launched the previous month, putting us one step closer to going to the moon. I believed in cause and effect, math, Newton's Laws, not in my father's world of premonitions and killer bridges. But I didn't want to disappoint him. I sometimes thought he was joking when he quoted Rod Serling's introduction to *The Twilight Zone*: "There is a fifth dimension beyond that which is known to man," he'd say, then tapping the side of his head and adding, "and I get signals from that dimension." Maybe his crazy predictions were a way of entertaining my mother and me. "Well," I said, waiting for him to crack a smile that would suggest he was just kidding.

"Listen," he said, stopping me. "I know your mother doesn't buy any of it, but you, you can keep an open mind, right?"

I wasn't sure. Maybe it was a joke, and, to keep him happy, I ought to go along with it. Before I could think of a safe answer, he sipped his beer and started off in a new direction. "So, tell me," he said, "what will you do, you know, after I'm gone."

"Dad, please." I didn't like to contemplate his dying. It was the beer talking. I squirmed and tried to think of an answer, one that would change the subject, take us to talking about Christmas or the Cleveland Browns. "I'll go to your funeral, and we'll bury you." I had wanted to sound flip, funny even, but my answer came out too serious, like I thought my father's death was imminent. I started to apologize.

"I won't get buried," he said.

"You want to be cremated?"

"No! I don't want to be grilled and roasted. My body ain't goin' to ever be found."

"Dad, I —"

"Shh, shh," he said, like he might be trying to calm a crying baby. "I need to know your plans," he said. "It'll give me peace of mind. You know how your whole life is supposed to flash before your eyes in that last second? I don't want that. When the bridge takes me, and I begin that long fall into the river, I want to see what you're going to be doing in the future."

The sun had set and beyond the plastic-covered windows the world was dark. "Well," I said, not knowing where to begin. "I'll go to college."

"Yeah, yeah, go on."

"Study science . . ."

"And write stories. You'll get that from me."

"Okay, I'll study physics and write stories."

"Girls?"

"Yeah, I'll study girls, too."

He slapped me on the knee. "Bet you will. I mean you going to get married and . . ."

"Maybe. Sure, I guess. When I find the right one or she finds me. We'll have two big dogs and go fishing somewhere up north every summer. I'll teach." I wasn't sure about the getting married or teaching part but thought the quicker we got over this the sooner we could talk about something else.

"This is good," he said. "Stay out of Vietnam. Okay, you'll do that?"

"Sure." I'd been considering enlisting in the army. Unless I got a scholarship the G.I. Bill was the only way I would be able to pay for college.

"And when you write your stories what will you say about me?"

I looked at him, the thick head of black hair growing a little gray around the temples, the hooked, hawk-like nose, the deep-set dark eyes, and the ears that resembled radar dishes. "That you are, were, a great dad. You came to all my basketball games."

"And your track meets," he said.

"And my track meets."

"Will you say how I tapped into that fifth dimension and had visions?"

I hesitated.

He pulled his feet off the windowsill. "Toes getting cold," he said.

A week later, the last time I saw my father he sat with his elbows on the breakfast table, sipping coffee from a cracked cup while reading the *Columbus Dis-*

patch. His black hair was an unruly mess, and his chin carried a dab of toilet paper to stem the blood from a fresh razor cut. After he finished his coffee, he folded the paper, stood up, grabbed his hat and coat, and headed toward the door. He was calling on a couple schools down the river and would be home early, in time to pick up a Christmas tree and come to my basketball game. "Good luck," he said. It was Friday, the 15th of December, and we planned to decorate our tree that weekend.

That evening was overcast with a northerly breeze carrying the odor of rotten eggs from power plants and steel plants upstream. Cars and trucks jammed on the bridge bumper-to-bumper. Tailpipes blew small, gray clouds, and cigarette smoke floated out partially cracked windows. The river ran fast and icy cold.

Drivers, impatient to get home to dinner or that night's high school basketball game between the Belpre Blue Devils and the Trimble Tomcats, sat on the bridge, hunched over their steering wheels, and fiddled with their radios as they waited for the light on the Ohio side to turn. Those listening to WWVA out of Wheeling heard Bing Crosby singing "White Christmas." Those tuned to WPKV listened to a news report that the war in Southeast Asia had spread to Laos. Even with the car windows rolled up against the December chill, everyone heard the bang. A suspension cable went slack. The bridge buckled and rolled. The north tower twisted and, like a giant tree after the final swing of an ax, began to fall.

Shopping bags carrying toy guns, dolls, flannel shirts, eight track tapes, and transistor radios—Christmas presents that had been on layaway since September—slipped off backseats. Jim McCarthy, feeling the earthquake-like shudder, feared a barge had struck one of the concrete pylons. Lily Rutowski, reapplying lipstick in the mirror, thought she'd bumped the car ahead of her. Myrna Tuck's first reaction was to grab the dinner plates she'd picked up at the pottery across the river, a wedding present for her niece. Dave George, sitting high in the cab of his Mack truck, looked over the tops of cars as they tumbled into the river while his best friend and partner, Leroy Newhouse, cut z's in the sleeper. Joe Brazitis, who had attended his first AA meeting that morning, was about to reach for the carefully wrapped bottle of Jim Beam sitting on the passenger seat of his Buick when he felt a higher power shake the bridge and stop him.

Uncle Zeke, a Korean War vet, nursing a cup of coffee at the lunch counter in Isaly's, flinched at the sound of what he thought was a mortar exploding. A West Virginia woman glancing out the window in anticipation of her husband coming home, cried out, Oh God! as she watched a young woman, a redhead without a coat, running past trapped cars as the bridge fell like a chain of dominoes behind her. The driver of an Omar Bakery truck ran down to the river and stared helplessly as a woman trapped in a slowly sinking car pounded on the driver's side window. A television repairman coming out of Dickey's Hardware claimed my father's station wagon, stuck in traffic midway across, caught his attention not because a pine tree was tied to the roof but because he knew my father refused to drive across the bridge.

My mother and I heard his story and others as we stood by the river, watching the crane pull cars out of the water, but we refused to believe my father had been on the bridge. "Television repairmen can't be believed," my mother said. Two days later they pulled Dad's blue Olds out of the river. Suspended from a long cable, it dangled and slowly turned like a giant mechanical fish. No body was inside.

Forty-six people died when the Silver Bridge collapsed. Two were never found. Over fifty years later I still visit the river every time I return home. I stand and listen to the water gurgle as it flows through the Japanese knotweed that has invaded the banks and try to tap into that hidden dimension my father claimed existed, a dimension, as Rod Serling used to say, of the imagination. I send messages to my dad, tell him that my future, much to my surprise, went pretty much as I had predicted. I didn't go to Vietnam, I became a science teacher, and, yes, I write stories. I tell him finding the love of my life took quite a few years, but I found her, and we have two giant dogs. I tell him I believe.

The water hisses and burbles along the bank.

Sometimes, I swear he answers.

Fireflies

After she finished radiation, after her scar had healed and a halo of curly, gold fuzz appeared on her head, my mother upgraded her fake breast. The previous one had been a little pad she slipped inside her bra, but the new one was better, "a foam rubber cutlet," she called it. For a week I had caught her prodding it with her fingertips at odd moments, a puzzled look on her face. Then, Saturday morning as I was getting ready to leave for work, she asked me to touch it, check it out. "Come here, Charlie," she said, planting herself in the middle of the kitchen doorway, her feet wide apart, blocking my escape.

I chewed on a slice of toast and stared at the maps she had pasted on the walls. Pennsylvania covered a two-foot-long strip above the stove. West Virginia hung next to the refrigerator, and Ohio, with a circle around Unity, was behind the dog's bowl, so, according to Mom, Trouble could find his way home if he ever got lost. She'd trimmed the maps carefully so that each one was the shape of the state and all other information, the list of counties and cities along with any pictures of state birds, flags, or flowers, was discarded. Every week for the past month, a new state had appeared, the route of a family vacation highlighted in the bright fluorescent green, blue or red my father had used when he planned the trip.

"Here," she repeated. She unbuttoned the top three buttons of her blouse and exposed the upper fringe of her bra. "Go ahead."

I touched Powder River Pass with the tip of my finger and followed the blue line while my mother stood in the door and waited. My father, mother and I had camped at Ten Sleep Creek the previous summer, and I was prepared to distract her with a question about when exactly the hailstorm hit or what my father had yelled when the black bear walked into the picnic grounds. I was seventeen, six foot four and weighed one eighty. I could throw a discus over a hundred and sixty feet and dunk a basketball two-handed behind my head, but I had not once poked, touched, rubbed, held, or caressed a breast, real or otherwise.

"Really," she said, "it won't hurt. No need to be shy. It's not me."
I leaned closer to Wyoming. Nothing on the map mentioned that some of the oldest rocks on Earth can be found in the Bighorn Mountains or that my father had thrown several dozen in the back of the pickup. Had he been alive--he was killed in the collapse of the Silver Bridge--my mother's request would have gone to him. And had my mother been dating--she wasn't--the job of checking out the breast might have gone to the boyfriend although I didn't like the idea of any man checking out my mother's breast, fake or not.

"Here," she persisted, poking it herself with a red fingernail. "See?"

A purple scar, still puckered and angry, ran up out of the bra toward her left shoulder. I glanced at the clock and then the door. "Maybe later," I said.

I worked in the park as a groundskeeper and spent most of my days riding the mower around the ball fields, the picnic grounds, and the basketball courts, far from the chatter and questions of those going to and from the pool. I was one of "Weaver's Crew," a group of high school students who shared a history of loss and misfortune. My father died in December, just two months later my mother found the lump in her breast. Greg's sister had been killed in a car accident three years earlier on the back road to Negley when a tool truck took a curve too fast and flipped into the oncoming lane. Kyle's brother was missing in Vietnam. The O'Hara twins, Coreen and Lyndsay, both lifeguards, came from a family of eleven. Their mother had been admitted to Youngstown's North Side Hospital for something the girls called "the blues." Mr. Weaver, the park supervisor, hired us because of our "special circumstances," and in return he got loyal workers and a sympathetic community that passed every park tax levy put on the ballot.

This was the summer of '69, the summer Charles Manson murdered Sharon Tate and six others, Senator Kennedy drove off a bridge, killing Mary Jo Kopechkne, Hurricane Camille, the strongest hurricane of the century, slammed into Mississippi, and the Vietcong launched a massive offensive on South Vietnam. The world was falling apart. Even before the next tragedy struck, we could feel its presence hanging in the air as heavy as the mosquito spray that lingered from the fogger's loop around the park the previous night. I worked alone and seldom talked with the others but when I did, we seldom discussed the news. We talked about our jobs: the temperature of the water in the pool, the mower deck's tendency to fall off, or the three dollars in change Coreen found at the bottom of the pool.

That Saturday morning, I was pruning the maples that lined the tennis courts, just watching the limbs fall, then moving on to the next. All morning little kids screamed and splashed in the wading pool while their mothers retrieved bright-colored plastic toys from the water. Young girls and boys threw insults back and forth, and every few minutes another car dropped off a load of kids. Limbs and branches piled up, and as the sun began to burn my shoulders I considered my mother's request. I'd driven her to Salem for chemo and radiation. I'd read the pamphlets in the waiting room describing various treatments and what could be expected after surgery. I'd seen clumps of her hair in the bathtub drain and listened to Mr. Ames, the high school counselor, whisper about the stages of grief while I sat in a hardback chair in his office and watched a wren flutter against the window. But nowhere had I heard or seen anything on the do's and do-nots of touching a mother's fake breast. I understood the possibility that she needed reassurance and that in some small way she might want me to take my father's place. I was no closer to figuring any of it out when around noon Coreen climbed down from her chair, and a tall blonde girl I'd never seen before climbed up. She crossed and uncrossed her long, tan legs, blew her whistle at a pale boy hanging on the ropes. I trimmed more trees, took my lunch alone in the shade, and continued to watch. Once, she glanced over in my direction, and I started to wave, but before I could lift my arm she looked away.

My best friend, Nick, was gone that summer, working on an uncle's hog farm in Iowa. I had no girlfriend. I spent my evenings shooting baskets at the hoop that hung from our garage or helping my mother paste another map on the kitchen walls. Sometimes, I'd rock on the front porch swing and listen to the trucks out on Route 14 or the music coming out of Miller's house two doors up. By a quarter-'til-four, I'd finished with the trees. The new girl was still there, so I waited until it was time for the hourly ten-minute break, then dropped my saw and walked over to the fence.

The air was heavy with the smell of chlorine, sun lotion and damp towels. Otis Redding's "Sittin on the Dock of the Bay" played on the loudspeakers that hung from the corners of the restrooms. The new lifeguard glanced in my direction, and I waved. She squinted, waved back. After everyone climbed out of the pool, she stepped down from her chair, dipped each foot in the water and walked over to the fence, leaving dark, wet footprints on the pale green paint. She swung the whistle in large circles with the practiced motion of a young girl turning a jump rope, but I guessed that she was my age, maybe a year older. Her black suit was faded and too small, the one, I suspect, she had worn the previous summer. A white strip of sunscreen ran the length of her nose. I wondered who she was and what misfortune her family had had.

I hooked my fingers through the chain link fence and leaned forward as if I was trying to pull it down. "Hey," I said, sawdust falling off my arms and out of my hair.

She smiled. "Why aren't you swimming?"

I shrugged. "I trim trees, mow."

She studied the oaks and maples that surrounded the pool, looking for cut limbs, frowning from the sun or maybe the thought of the damage I might be doing to nature.

Her name was Jennifer Morgan and her family had moved into a farmhouse on the back road to Waterford. They came to Ohio to be closer to grandparents, but she missed her friends back in Minnesota and said she hoped to go back to visit them at the end of summer. As we talked, she repeatedly pulled on the straps of her suit, lifting one side, then the other, and I pretended not to notice her breasts moving and swelling under the shifting pressure. I looked up at the clouds and over at the pile of limbs next to the tennis court. I looked down at her feet and at the kids lining up at the edge of the pool, but then she'd tug again on the straps and the strip of pale skin pushing over the top of her suit would catch my eye.

Before she headed back to her chair, I asked if I could pick her up when she got off work, take her out for a milkshake, and she said, yes.

When I arrived home, my mother was standing in the kitchen next to Montana, a bright red scarf tied around her head, the tip of her finger tracing a blue line while she sipped a glass of iced tea. Although still very thin, she had gained weight and lost the dark circles beneath her eyes. "Your dad and I were in Missoula," she said. "In a nature store that sold posters and photographs of grizzly bears. That was their thing, grizzly bears. They had clay models of them and life-sized casts of their paws. There was even a stuffed bear in the corner, maybe seven-foot tall, with yellow teeth and sharp claws. Your dad was staring at it when this huge black dog came up behind him and licked his hand. He yelled and almost jumped over the counter. He thought it was a bear." She tapped the map with her fingertip and chuckled. "You should know these things." Her hand went to her breast.

"I have a date," I said.

She looked down at the front of her blouse. "They come in every size you could possibly want."

"Your new one looks good," I said. "You'd never know."

She shook her head. "Boobs."

I looked at Montana. "I could stay home."

She ran the palm of her hand over the map. "Who?"

"A lifeguard, a new girl. Jennifer Morgan. I won't be late."

She looked at her watch. "You don't want to see them land on the moon?"

"Maybe at Jennifer's," I said.

"Jenn--i--fer," my mother said, drawing out each syllable. "The new family?"

I nodded.

She frowned, started to say something, and stopped.

"I can be home early," I said.

She glanced at the map, then back at me. "No, no. We've talked about this. " She dropped her arms straight to her sides. "I look like a wooden matchstick, don't I?"

I studied her. White slacks, white blouse, pale skin, the red scarf on her head. "Like you could burst into flames any minute," I said.

My mother having breast cancer and my dad dying a week before Christmas would have gotten my mother the sympathy vote from everyone in town, but she wouldn't have any of it. "No pity party here," she said. She made jokes about paying half price for her next breast exam, and once, when she grew dissatisfied with the fake breast, threw it out, saying, "Wait until you see my new knocker."

Before I left for Jennifer's, my mother called me back into the kitchen and pointed at the map of New Hampshire next to the door. "This is where we picked apples," she said, pointing at a little dot. "Cortland, the best."

I stared at the green line my father had traced through Franconia Notch, Mount Washington, and Lincoln. There was a photograph on the living room bookcase of the two of them backpacking in the White Mountains. He was a traveling salesman, selling floor wax and other cleaning supplies to schools, and in the picture she's eighteen, just weeks out of high school. Her brown hair hangs halfway down her back. His arm is in the air, about to wrap around her shoulder, his worn, brown backpack at his feet. He'd balanced the camera on a nearby rock and raced back to embrace her, but he was a fraction of a second too slow and the camera had caught his arm in midair.

"Oh, the places we went," she said.

Had I not been going out, I would have pointed at the map of West Virginia and asked if she remembered camping at Cheat Lake. She would have described how my father had backpacked a pizza four miles to our campsite and asked if I remembered feeding the squirrels the burnt crust.

She looked forward to watching the astronauts walk on the moon later that evening and it didn't seem right that she should be alone. I hesitated at the door.

"I'll be fine," she said.

A brown dust cloud billowed behind the truck as I drove down the dirt road to Jennifer's. Small stones flew up through the hole in the floorboard and road maps my mother had not yet found flapped beneath the seat. Each time I hit a rut or bounced on the washboard, the billion-year-old Wyoming rocks bounced and banged in the truck bed. The rocks were rough and gray, nothing special to look at, but my father had liked the idea that they were among the oldest rocks on Earth, and he had wanted to make a border around the flower garden in our backyard with them.

Jennifer had said she lived next to an abandoned semi-trailer, so when I saw the graffiti decorated trailer, I figured that was her place. The front porch sloped like the deck of a sinking ship and the yard was wild with bushes and shrubs that hadn't been trimmed in years. I turned into the drive and killed the ignition. The engine coughed, then died as I ran up the front steps, rang the door-bell and waited. In a far room of the house a woman sang "Somebody loves you, peek over here… " She had a good voice and I waited until she paused before ringing again. A few seconds later a barefoot woman wearing a necklace of bright colored beads opened the door.

"Yes?" she asked.

"I'm Charlie," I said.

She stared at me like we'd already met, and she was trying to remember my name or take in how I'd changed. Then she tipped her head, smiled, and opened the door for me to step inside. "Charlie Wright," she said, not as a way of saying hi, but like the name meant something, which I hoped was a good thing. I tucked my hands under my arms, then shoved them in my jean pockets. I felt awkward. Jennifer's mother was younger than I had expected, and it was my first date in close to a year. I stepped into her living room where a fan, rotating on the floor, shot a blast of warm air my way every few seconds. A pink sweater was draped across the banister. "Nice evening," I said.

The fan turned and her blouse fluttered as if a bird trapped inside was trying to get out.

"A little warm," she said, looking at me as if I might be selling something, which, I suppose, I was. She had curly, red hair and a white eyebrow that gave her a skeptical, flirting look. She was barefoot and had that comfortable with her body look many hippies had. I couldn't see any resemblance between Jennifer and her mother, but I wasn't good at spotting that sort of thing. I liked the white eyebrow.

I agreed it was warm and said one of the advantages of working at the park was being allowed to swim after the pool closed. I asked if she swam and she said yes, but she burned easily. She pointed at her red hair.

"My mother's hair is coming in curly," I said, thinking that this woman, although new to town, might know my mother. She gave me a blank look and I scrambled to explain. "The radiation. It all fell out."

She ran her fingers through her hair and grinned. "The red is mine, but the curls are not."

The bare feet, the beads, and that white eyebrow were throwing me off. I stepped back, crossed my arms against my chest. I suspected she was sizing me up, wondering what sort of guy was going out with her daughter. I told her about my job at the park and how during my lunch break I shot hoops at the basketball court or sat in the shade and watched a family of black squirrels chase each other up and down the trunks of the trees. We talked about the astronauts who were then just hours away from walking on the moon. She listened intently, nodding, cocking her eyebrow, biting her lip, and opening her eyes wide.

We stood there for another minute discussing the weather (hot and dry) and what a terrible summer it was for the Cleveland Indians (last place) while I wondered what Jennifer was doing. I glanced at the sweater draped over the banister. "Jennifer?" I asked

"Jennifer?" The woman repeated.

I felt as if I'd been dropped on another planet. "Jennifer Morgan?"

She shook her head.

I went out onto the front porch and looked up and down the road. I half expected to see Jennifer waving from a distant drive, but she was nowhere in sight. The woman stood behind the screen door and watched. "The new family?" I asked.

She smiled, leaned out, and pointed at a gray house a hundred yards up the road.

This time, I left the engine running while I hurried to the front door and knocked. A black cat, sunning on the porch, arched its back and tiptoed away. I knocked again and pressed my nose to the screen. A television flickered. A folded wheelchair and a green oxygen tank stood near the end of a sofa. I was debating whether I should call out and ask if anyone was home when Jennifer danced down the steps. As she opened the front door she turned and called out, "Be back later," but no one answered.

I was about to explain the problem I'd had with her directions when she interrupted. "I don't normally go out with guys I don't know, but you look safe."

Safe? Pinky Lee was safe. Buffalo Bob and Soupy Sales were safe. Look at how many dates they got. Probably none. I was almost twenty. I did not want to be safe. "Hungry?" I asked, trying unsuccessfully to inject a little menace in my voice.

A car flew by, sending up a cloud of dust that drifted toward us.

Jennifer coughed, waved her hand, choked, and turned away from the road. "You betcha," she said. She'd changed into black shorts and a black tank top, and when she slid into the truck, a black bra strap slipped off her shoulder.

On the way to town, she played with the radio knob. "Bob Dylan is from Minnesota," she said. She paused to gauge my reaction. "Zimmerman is his real name. We're distantly related."

"I like his songs," I said, although I couldn't always understand the lyrics. Jennifer seemed pleased, but she found only static and a baseball game. She shrugged, leaned back, and smiled. "Ohio," she said, staring out the window at a wooded hillside where my father and I had once gone mushroom hunting. Her hair blew in her face, and she pulled long fine strands from her mouth. When we stopped at the crossing on Blair Road for a slow-moving train, she offered me a stick of Black Jack gum, then held her hand under my nose. "I smell like chlorine," she said. Her bare knee rocked back and forth, coming dangerously close to the gear shift and my hand.

"That's okay," I said. The train passed, and we waved at the two men standing on the back of the caboose. As I drove across the tracks, she ran her hand over the seat and glanced through the rear window at the rocks rattling around in the rusted bed. "Nice truck."

I looked to make sure she wasn't joking. The upholstery was cracked and peeling off the seats, there was a hole in the floorboard next to the clutch, and the dome light dangled from a single black wire like a giant spider about to drop between us.

"Thanks," I said, "it was my father's."

She stuck out her lower lip and nodded as if she approved.

"He died."

"Sorry," she said, running her fingers through her hair, untangling knots.

I waited for her to ask how he died, but she didn't. "He never trusted the bridge," I said. "He said it was going to kill him and it did." Still, Jennifer didn't ask any questions. Maybe she wasn't worried about dying herself, maybe she was and didn't want any details on how easily it could happen. Or maybe how didn't matter.

"I'm starving," she said again. She twisted a cheap ring with a yellow stone on her finger. I felt sorry for her, but I wasn't sure why.

We were the only ones in the Fiesta Drive-In parking lot, everyone else probably home watching the lunar landing. We sipped our shakes and listened to the sizzle and snap of the blue electric bug zapper that hung above a picture of a giant chocolate cone outside Jennifer's window. She said she knew all the words to Dylan's songs and that in Minnesota he was bigger than the Beatles. Her black bra strap slipped farther down her arm. It looked smooth and silky, and I wondered if that was one of the things my mother missed. Perhaps white bras with pockets for a fake breast didn't feel the same. Jennifer joked about a boy at the pool who had lost his suit when he dove off the board and had cried so hard she was afraid he was going to drown. I started to tell her about my dad and me swimming in a mountain stream, but I stopped, realizing it had nothing to do with a boy losing his pants.

Jennifer said that the men in her hometown went ice fishing every winter and three of her friends camped out one night when it was thirty below. "That's what it's like there," she said. She fiddled with the radio knob. "What's a buckeye?" she asked, but before I could explain she looked at her watch. "If we hurry, we could watch them walk on the moon."

"Sure," I said, backing out of the drive-in, then adding, "It's a kind of nut."

I was racing down the back road to Waterford, listening to the billion-year-old rocks bounce in the back, when I got the idea of showing one to Jennifer when we got to her house. I'd tell her about Ten Sleep Creek and how my father and I had collected those rocks during a hailstorm, but, before I could start my story, there was a loud thump. The entire windshield bounced. Jennifer shrieked. Blood and feathers splattered everywhere.

I hit the brakes and the body of a large bird slid off the hood. Jennifer stared at the windshield. Her face was white, and her mouth hung open. I wasn't sure if she was breathing. "Jennifer?" I said.

She didn't move.

"Jennifer?"

She buried her face in her hands and moaned. "You should have swerved," she said. "You should have been watching."

I got out of the truck and walked back to where the bird lay beside the road. The large round eyes were open, and one wing was stretched out as if trying to fly, but it didn't move. I nudged it with the toe of my shoe, then rolled it into the ditch. When I got back in the truck, Jennifer was sobbing. "An owl," I said.

She choked, and I thought she was going to be sick. I turned on the wipers, but they only smeared the blood. Jennifer groaned again. "Sorry," I said. I rolled down the window and leaned out in order to see down the road. I didn't know what else to say. It came out of nowhere.

She wiped her eyes and stared at her feet, so she wouldn't see the blood or feathers. "Didn't you see it?" she asked. Then she was quiet until we turned into her drive, and I asked if there was hose I could use to clean the windshield.

She pointed to the side of the house. "There." She opened the front door and went inside.

I found the hose in the weeds, but the nozzle didn't work, and I couldn't get much pressure. Feathers slid across the hood and caught under the wipers, splatters of blood clung to the side mirror, and I got almost as wet as the truck. But eventually, the windshield was clean enough for me to drive home. After I rewound the hose, I went to the front steps, and Jennifer appeared on the other side of the screen door. "I'm sorry," she said.

"Me too," I said. Then she closed the door.

If there had been no owl, if I could have told Jennifer about my mother pasting the maps to the wall and how difficult it was for her to raise her arm. Jennifer would have invited me inside, and we would have sat close to each other on her couch. She would have told me more about Minnesota and Bob Dylan. She would have rested her head on my shoulder, and we would have leaned into each other while we watched the astronauts walk on the moon.

That is, I think, the way things sometimes get started.

As it was, I climbed into the truck and backed slowly out of Jennifer's drive. Drops of water ran down the windshield and rolled across the hood. The porch light went out. I waved in case anyone was watching, then headed down the road. As I passed the old farmhouse, I saw the woman with the white eyebrow sitting on the porch steps. She waved with a flutter of her fingers, and I realized she'd probably known all along that I was at the wrong house. I stopped, backed up, then pulled forward until I was off the road. I didn't know whether to turn off the engine and lights, but she scooted over and patted the steps, so I did.

"You knew I was at the wrong house, didn't you?" I asked as I walked up the weed-lined path.

She grinned. "I suspected."

"And you didn't say anything."

She shook her head.

"You let me walk right in. I could have been a dangerous man." I leaned against the wood railing that ran up the side of the steps doing my best mysterious-dangerous guy imitation. "And don't say I look safe."

"You've never been safe," she said.

I tried to remember when we might have met but was pretty sure I'd have remembered a pretty woman with a white eyebrow. I slowly shook my head, a signal I was thinking but coming up short.

"It's been a while."

I wondered if she'd been at my father's funeral. Dozens of people I didn't know paraded by, looked at the photos on the table, slapped me on the shoulder, grabbed my hand, said what a tragedy and how much they'd miss him. Still, there are some faces I would have remembered and hers was one.

"From a previous life," she said.

Before I could ask, she glanced at my jeans. The white eyebrow went up.

"I hit an owl," I said. And then I explained that I'd had to wash off the truck, so I could see out the windshield. "I got wet, too."

She nodded as if it all made perfect sense. "It was probably diving for a mouse," she said.

I stood there thinking I should get home but not really wanting to go.

"Why aren't you watching the landing?"

She pointed at the field. "Have a seat and enjoy the show."

Across the road, fireflies, more fireflies than I'd ever seen, hovered over fresh cut hay. Soft yellow lights drifted in every direction, blinking in a secret language only fireflies understood. I sat on the step, the air smelling of powder and shampoo.

She smiled. "Want a Coke?"

It was after ten. My mother was home alone, perhaps trying to paste a new map to the cupboards.

"Ice cold."

And what next if I said no? Watching the fireflies across the road and sitting next to a woman I did not know, I thought the whole world seemed delicately balanced, and at the right time a small shove might get it spinning in the right direction.

"Sure," I said.

She pushed herself up, one hand braced against my shoulder, and went inside. I stared at the quarter moon hanging above the trees at the edge of the field and thought of the tiny space capsule nearly two hundred thousand miles away. Then the screen door creaked, and she was sitting beside me again.

"You waiting for someone?" I asked as she handed me the bottle.

A car went down the road, and we both watched until the red taillights disappeared in the distance. "Not tonight," she said. Then, "Charley?"

"Yes?" I answered, surprised she remembered my name.

She stuck out her hand, "I'm Charlene. I'm a Charlie, too."

And sometimes, this is how things get started: A teenage boy and a woman with a white eyebrow, two Charlies, a cold Coke, and a night full of fireflies. She reached out and caught one, but when she opened her fingers, it refused to fly away. It blinked on and off in her hand, its pale-yellow light illuminating the lines that ran across her palm like tiny highways.

"Want to hear an old rock story?" I asked.

She tossed the lightning bug into the air. "You bet."

"From Wyoming," I said. "Three billion years old."

She nodded, then pulled her knees up and wrapped her hands around her ankles.

I went to the truck and picked up a fist-sized rock for her to see. "Gneiss," I said, handing it to her. She turned it over and pressed it against her cheek. I sat down beside her, sipped my Coke, and took a deep breath. And then I told her how my father and I had jumped into Cheat Lake and the water was so cold we could barely move. She said she had once gone swimming beneath a mountain waterfall and had nearly frozen, her skin going numb until it felt like plastic. We traded stories back and forth, our voices growing softer as we watched the moon sink behind the trees, her shoulder pressed against mine. Frogs croaked in a nearby pond and an owl, perhaps looking for its mate, hooted from a distant tree.

THE UNCERTAINTY PRINCIPLE

How Coal Was Formed

The moon floats fat, white, and tempting over the abandoned strip mines outside your bedroom window. *Come on up, Zeke. I dare you. I double dare.* Like the barker at last summer's street fair, the one calling, "Step up! Three balls for a dollar. Win a teddy bear for your girl."

You uncorked your fast ball and got the teddy bear with one pitch, and the barker asked you to not play again.

The moon rising slowly, a big bubble. Come on.

Kennedy said we'd do it, go to the moon and back, but it's going to be a race. The USSR has been launching rockets faster than Tubby Parker's old man can light the Fourth of July fireworks behind the baseball diamond in the park. Russian dogs and cosmonauts spinning around the Earth, passing overhead, while our rockets popped and fizzled, blew up, and fell down, but we're catching up, gaining ground, gaining space so to speak. We've got the Saturn V and lordy, lordy, that firecracker is big. Five engines. Seven and a half million pounds of thrust. Climb in, buckle up, sit on enough rocket fuel to, well, to blow you from here to the moon. Cramped capsule, g-forces, weightlessness, radiation, expense be damned.

The moon. Almost two hundred thousand miles one way, more miles than you've got on your '57 Chevy, cruising around town with the window down, your elbow out, baseball cap pushed back, nodding at the girls, flashing your smile. You imagine the rocket's roar and someone, a spaceman, an astronaut, sticking the stars and stripes there on the surface and everyone feeling proud, walking tall, chests stuck out, thinking, By God, we did it, where we going next?

One week from graduation and the draft, and you lie in bed loving life while your brother across the room worries about you don't know what. You can't sleep for his complaining. Problems in East Germany, Africa, Cuba, Korea. Trouble everywhere, he says. Soldiers going to Southeast Asia. The commies must be stopped and better in those jungle places than Hawaii or at the Golden Gate Bridge. But Les isn't going to Southeast Asia. Asthma.

You don't say it, can't say it, but you feel guilty for secretly seeing Holly, your brother's girlfriend. She says you are the wild one.

You dance fast, drive fast, throw the baseball even faster, but that doesn't make you wild, or so what if it does.

You wonder if Holly feels guilty, too. You worry your brother—who never drives fast, dances fast, or swears—might discover what you and Holly have going. Les says he loves Holly so much she doesn't need to love him back, but he doesn't understand. Holly is in love with you, and if you keep thinking about her, you'll never go to sleep. Long-legged, dimple-cheeked, toe-tapping Holly. Holly who said she was a bit flat-chested before she let your hand creep up under her blouse, and you said it was okay, it didn't matter, that you liked flat-chested, that you didn't think she was. Saying everything, anything, hoping something would sound right.

"Go to sleep," your brother says over the banter of Johnny Carson and Ed McMahon on the other side of the wall, from the only black and white set left in all Ohio in maybe the only house in the state without indoor plumbing.

"What was that noise?" he asks.

"Nothing," you say.

You don't hear any noise. "Blinking," you say. "I was blinking."

"Go to sleep," he says, your older brother who is afraid to run down to the outhouse in the middle of the night.

You pop a knuckle.

"Go to sleep," he says, your brother with radar ears.

Holly lives across the state line in Darlington. You like that she lives in Pee-A, in the town of *Darling*….ton. You think about her laugh and then about her breasts and the weight of them in your hands. How smooth the skin. She's perfect, and you never thought a flat breast could feel so good. You hold your hand above the sheets and try to imagine their softness and warmth.

You imagine Holly's breast in your mouth and get an instant erection there under the sheets. You grab it and think, whoa, Saturn V, then wish she was there beside you, which wouldn't be good what with your brother, her so-called boyfriend, only a few feet away.

The moon creeps higher over the stripper cuts, the scarred and scabbed-over land where the giant shovels and drag lines of Ferris Coal pushed and scraped the topsoil aside and stripped out a seam of bituminous more than three feet thick. The cuts go for miles in all directions, nothing but hills of crumbling shale and broken rock, a few scrub pine and stunted sumac clinging to the steep slopes of loose stone, at night, sometimes you and Holly in the backseat of the Chevy, hiding among the shadows.

The moon, smooth, pale, and round, floats just beyond your reach. Tempting. Like Natalie Wood giving you the wink. A real tease.

Your brother hates it here, hates the outhouse, hates the cuts, hates living on a small farm. It embarrasses him. You wouldn't trade it for all the cigarettes in Ohio. The cuts border one side of the farm and fields and woods border it on the other. What's not to love?

And then Saturday morning sun shining on the wall, illuminating the maps of the places you've never been. Wyoming. Montana. Idaho. Quickly, you pull on a pair of jeans, a T-shirt, and grab a couple slices of bread on your way out the door. Your brother is still asleep. For you, a clean escape.

You jog into the stripper cuts behind the house, not slowing down until you're out of sight, standing at the edge of a cut that has filled with water. White cumulus clouds hang in a pale blue sky, their reflection floating on the surface of the pond, the water deep and cold. In three hours, you'll be baling hay but first a morning swim. You kick off your shoes thinking about Holly and the way she traces the veins on the back of your hands with her fingernail. It's a wonder you can do anything, the way she's taken over your thoughts. You need to buy condoms. But Holly might be angry if she saw one in your wallet, and she had no intention of doing anything. It would be like you were taking the doing it for granted.

You think she has intentions.

The last time you shot pool with Tubby, he showed you his brother's shoebox half full of condoms. One brand called "PRIME" came in bright red packages promising extra sensitivity, and you memorized the name. Then that very Sunday Reverend Emerick stood in the pulpit and said how everyone would mourn the loss of their dear friend Red Carter, "who died in his prime." You and Tubby started snickering. It was bad to laugh when the congregation was praying for Red's family and his soul, but you did. The laugh came out in tight, little spurts, and even now, sitting next to the pond, you chuckle. A man in his Prime. Just as you are about to drop your jeans and dive in, a van pulls up with college students and a professor.

They've been here before and you've followed along, listened to what the professor had to say, and the students had to ask. Neither of the two girls are as pretty as Holly, but you watch and smile as they follow the boys and the professor up the side of a cut. You put your shoes back on, walk over, stand near the group, and listen to the professor's coal formation stories: swamps and trees, dragonflies the size of seagulls, organic matter trapped between two layers, millions and millions of years.

The professor gestures at the surrounding area. "The cuts disrupted the water table, and some of the old farmhouses still don't have indoor plumbing," he says. "The wells can't produce enough water." He sees you and catches himself too late.

You want to shout that your family has a two-hole outhouse, but you don't. You're cool. A man of few words.

Then he says there are rumors of a nudist camp across the line, over in Pennsylvania, hidden among the miles of stripper cuts. That a nudist camp might exist in the stripper cuts seems perfect for a joke. A few of the boys turn and look, smiles on their faces, hoping to see what? A naked woman playing tennis, her hand stretched high above her head as she stands on her toes, waiting to return a serve?

You know where it is. You and Tubby sat on top one of the hills at dusk, passing binoculars back and forth while peering down inside the sheet metal fence that surrounded The Sunshine Club. Art Hill, who owns the sports store on Main Street, and Grace Bird, the leggy teller at the bank, were playing croquet, and although you were too far away to hear the click of the wooden balls, the binoculars brought Grace up close. When she bent over the ball, you thought you would explode or burst into flames, your eyes glued to Grace until Tub yanked the binoculars out of your hands.

One of the college boys says the stripper cuts look like something from the moon. "If we're going to send people to the moon, they should practice here," he says. The rest of the class waits for the professor's comment, waits to laugh, but the professor looks around, smiles, squints up at the sun.

The boy shifts his weight, sends a piece of broken shale down the hillside. The students watch the rock as it tumbles, kicks up puffs of dust and triggers a little landslide. The rock plops into the water, and the professor turns back to the students, tries to remember what he was going to say.

Next to the cut where you swim there's a pile of rusted-out refrigerators, broken televisions, old bed springs and a mountain of trash. Last fall, your father poured gasoline on the garbage, lighted a rag he'd tied to a cornstalk and twirled the torch through the air. The flames shot ten, twenty feet high. Aerosol cans and bicycle inner tubes popped and exploded, and black smoke curled into the sky and drifted east toward Beaver Falls and Darlington. The heat pressed against your face and the front of your jeans even though you were standing at the top of the hill, far enough away to be safe from the exploding cans.

Your old man told you and Les to shoot the rats as they tried to escape the flames.

Les never pulled the trigger, but you nailed four rats.

Later, after the flames died down, your hair reeked of smoke and garbage, and you dived into that deep cut and swam in water so cold it numbed your toes. You swam on top of an upside-down universe, the stars burning below, the cold water rippling above. You swam back and forth until you no longer smelled the garbage or heard the squealing rats. You swam until you felt that by letting go, you could fall forever.

Your mom doesn't like the smoke or the way the odor finds its way into the house and sticks to the sofa and stuffed chair. She doesn't like what it might do to the air or the water where you swim.

Your brother doesn't swim in the pond. He doesn't drink or swear. You think he might be too good, that he judges you for the fun you have.

But this morning there are no rats, just the professor and the students. The air is clear, the sun is rising, the grass is growing, and, like the cosmonauts, astronauts, and the draftees, you have places to go. As you run down the hill and back up the road, you catch a fleeting glimpse of one girl watching you, smiling. You wave.

The night before you leave for basic training you and Holly do it. No Prime. You've done it with other girls, and you loved every one of them but none as much as you love Holly. Protection is like showering with your raincoat on, you think, but this time you wonder if your luck might have run out. It's just a feeling, a hunch, a premonition.

Months later, on patrol near An Khe, the moon is full, so bright you can read the letter you've saved all day as easily as if you were sitting on a sandy South Sea beach at sunset. You rest on your poncho, lace your fingers beneath your head, stare at the night sky and feel as if you're floating. You swear when you get home the first thing you're going to do, even before you see Holly, is jump in the cut behind the house and float there, wash away the smell and sounds of this place. You don't care how cold the water is. You don't care if those college kids are lined up ten deep watching. You're going to strip and dive in. And damn, it's going to feel good.

You carefully open Holly's letter. You have that hunch that your luck has run out, and there might be bad news inside that will bite you. Sure enough, there it is in her slanted cursive. She's pregnant. She doesn't say, "It's yours," but you think it might be. The timing is right, and you can't imagine your brother being responsible. She and Les are going to get married. A punch to the gut. Does your brother know you might be the father? You think you should answer the letter, but do you congratulate them, say you're sorry, or ask Holly to wait until you get home? You don't know what to say, so you write nothing.

A distant oxen bell clangs, and then, as if on cue, a heavy fog rolls in. The moon disappears. The air is so thick with heat, humidity, and homesickness, you think you're going to drown.

And then you're humping toward Pleiku, returning from a patrol in the Central Highlands, the red soil of Vietnam like powder beneath your feet. You don't know how you got here, but here you are and it's hotter than it ever got back in Ohio. Hotter than any place you've ever been. You think about Holly, but the heat makes it difficult. What you want more than anything is to fall in the stripper cut behind your house. You and Holly. Yeah, that works. You and Holly under a full moon, skinny dipping. You're really getting into it, the cool water sliding up your legs, Holly floating toward you in the moonlight. But Holly is your brother's pregnant wife and the image fades.

As you enter the clearing at the edge of a rice paddy, a tiny breeze tickles your neck. You wait, hope for it to build into something stronger, but it doesn't. Just hot air, maybe someone's breath. Four hundred meters across a narrow earthen dike to the tree line. Five klicks from camp. Home free almost. Corey walking point. Nebraska boy leading the platoon. A cornhusker with a girlfriend named Holly. Corey and his Holly are getting married when he gets back home, going to have the reception and dance in the barn. He threw his head back when telling you and grinned with those big Nebraska teeth. "I can smell the hay," he said.

You stare at the dark stain of sweat on Corey's back. He's got the farm boy walk, a carefree stroll across a plowed field. You glance up at the sky, hoping to see a cloud that might block the sun, when there's a thud and the bark of a rifle and then all hell.

Everyone hits the ground, hugs the side of the dike except Corey who is walking up ahead like nothing happened, like he's zoned to a different world. You're about to shout his name when you see the dark red spot blooming on his back. Slugs slap into the muddy dike and spit in the water. There are grunts and groans and shouts of "Medic!" "On the left, on the left!" "In the trees!" "Medic!" A sharp pain in your stomach. You grab, afraid your hand will come away sticky or find a hole, but it's only the first aid pouch pinching your skin. The VC are there on the other side of the paddy, but you can't see how many. They're behind the trees and, God, you hope there aren't more somewhere else.

But Corey is out there walking, one step after the other, like nothing has happened. Like he's invincible except for the blood running down his back, dripping on the red dirt.

You can't believe he hasn't dropped for cover. You yell, "Corey!"

He hesitates, stops as if he's thinking, then his left leg buckles, and he falls.

"Corey," you yell. "Corey!" You run out and are pulling him back behind the dike when he slips out of your hand. You look down. Part of your hand is missing, and it doesn't even hurt, not yet, even though there's a lot of blood. Then a sharp pain in your shoulder and that does hurt. You fall on top of Corey and hug the dike.

Goose bumps run up and down your back like an electric current, and it must be two hundred fucking degrees. Corey isn't moving. Maybe you broke his concentration, maybe, if you'd kept quiet, he could have kept on walking. Bullets snap overhead. Lieutenant Reesh with Fritz, the RTO, on the horn yelling for support, saying two have been hit and you're pinned down. Sonofabitch.

Beanie, the medic calls out to you, says, "Hang on, Easy." None of the guys call you Ezekiel or Zeke, which you like. Yeah, you think, that's me, Easy.

The others fire into the trees while Lurch crawls along the dike with the M-60. You're scared and you hate lying in the stinking water up to your neck. You push forward an inch and your boots sink in the muck. Then Lurch opens fire, and tracers streak across the paddy, shooting stars beneath a cloudless sky.
Limbs and green vegetation fall to the ground. *Splat, splat.* Two slugs bury themselves in the dike near your head. One by one the others are backing up, crawling toward Lurch and the cover of the trees. Then Beanie, the medic, pops up with his good-luck feather taped to the side of his helmet and presses a large pad against your shoulder, wraps your hand says, "You're going to be okay."

You don't feel okay, but you take his word for it. "Corey," you say.

There's the batbatbat of the M-60 and the clank of empty cartridges as Lurch fires across the paddy, aiming the machinegun like a fireman trying to hose down a fire, but as soon as one spot in the trees goes quiet, another spot flares up. Lurch pauses for a second, letting the barrel of the M-60 cool. Beanie, bent over

Corey, says, "Fuck, fuck, fuck."

Sweat runs down your face and drips off your chin. You're afraid of dying, of never seeing Holly again. You try to picture her face, but the image won't form. You hate the VC and the fuck-ups who thought today's leg would be an easy hump. You wipe your face with the back of your hand and feel a soft, slippery mass, a fucking leech. You try to scrape it off, but it clings to your cheek. The dike is low, offering only minimal protection and the mud and muck make it tough going, but, slowly, you crawl back toward Lurch and the others. Lurch fires across the paddy, but the VC move from one place to another. As soon as it seems safe to run, a bullet snaps overhead or in the water on the other side of the dike. You slide back down into the paddy. A bad place to die, you think, trying again to swipe the leech from your face with your bandaged hand.

You listen and pray for the thump, thump of choppers. You can almost feel the VC tiptoeing around in those black pajamas or maybe setting the angle on mortar tubes, getting ready to drop a couple on you.

Then jets. One up high, circling, while the other screams in at treetop and drops a load, muffled pops that sound like the aerosol cans exploding in your father's fires. Flames leap up and out, burn the trees and shrubs, even the red dirt. A hundred meters away but you feel the heat, you smell it.

The shooting stops. No birds singing. No mosquitoes buzzing. Only the sound of the mud and muck sucking at your feet, the crackling of flames, and the jets climbing in the distance, the afterburners a bright white glow.

You look at Corey stretched out along the dike and wonder if he'd been thinking about home, about walking down a dirt lane holding hands with Holly, and after the bullet passed through his chest he couldn't die because he was someplace else. Maybe he felt the bullet, but he wouldn't let go of Holly's hand or the smell of hay. Maybe he was thinking that if he and Holly reached the end of the lane everything would be okay.

While recovering, you try writing left-handed to Corey's Holly, tell her Corey was thinking about her, talking about the reception in the barn when it happened, but then you throw the scribbles away and try writing your Holly, your brother's Holly instead. You throw that letter away, too. Later, the night is so dark you're afraid to stretch your arms out in front of you, afraid of who or what you might touch.

You get letters from home. Tubby writes and says he saw your brother and his wife sharing milkshakes at Huck's Dairy. Holly was holding a baby girl. Do you want your brother killed?

You wonder what the little girl looks like, if she resembles you, but it's the cold milkshakes they were drinking that you can't get out of your mind.

Your mother writes and says they bought a color TV, and your father singed his eyebrows while burning the trash, but he's okay. You wonder why your folks waited until you left to buy the color TV. Your mom includes a list of every dead or dying person in town, says your dad is doing fine. Sometimes he writes "Take Care" at the bottom of the letters. You get letters from Marvella, Cindy, and Annie, other girls you loved, but you do not hear again from Holly.

You feel bad and angry about losing Holly but think it's partly your fault. You couldn't hold her in your mind, think about her when it was hot or when you were wading through muck or pulling leeches as big as pocketknives off your neck. You couldn't hold your Holly in your mind the way Corey could hold his.

You lose two years, two friends, two fingers, twenty pounds, and your grandfather's good-luck silver dollar, but you are one of the lucky ones. You keep your legs, arms, and balls, and then, just like that, you're standing in the Youngstown airport with a duffel bag slung over your good shoulder and two hundred bucks in your pocket, a rich man, looking for your father.

You're shaky. Too much caffeine. Jet-lag. The body waiting to get jumped. Your father shows up more stoop-shouldered than you remember. His black hair is streaked with gray and going thin. You give each other a one-armed bear hug, and he says it's good to see you. He glances at your hand and quickly looks away. He seems nervous, disappointed, and you wonder if he was always like this, and you just hadn't noticed. On the drive home you sit and stare out the window. He talks and talks, says your brother has some hard feelings, real hard feelings.

He drives you around town, pointing at the new scoreboard erected at one end of the high school football field and then swings by the former vacant lot now home of a McDonalds. "Progress," he says. He then takes you home, pulls in front of the barn and points at a trailer set back in the woods. "You can stay there if you want, a place of your own until . . . you know." Your mom hugs you, kisses you on the cheek, bakes a chocolate cake with caramel icing, and insists she's going to put some fat back on your bones.

Everything is awkward. It's as if nothing fits or you and your parents no longer speak the same language. They pretend not to look at your hand, at the missing fingers, and your father grimaces when he catches sight of your bare shoulder.

"You're quiet," they say again and again. They give each other looks and whisper when they think you can't hear. Maybe they didn't expect you to come home or they liked it better when you weren't around.

You move into the trailer beyond the barn, thinking it's only temporary although you like it there, the quiet.

Your father promised they'd have indoor plumbing by the time you got home, but the well wasn't producing enough water. Still, it's summer, and you're home, and you head out to the cuts, planning to drop your pants, kick off your shoes, fall in, paddle around and let the fish nibble on your fingers. Your father follows you, asks again how you're doing.

"Okay," you say again.

When you get to the cut, the water is covered with green scum that came from you don't know fucking where or what. "What the fuck?" you say, and your old man looks embarrassed, jams his hands in his pockets, says it's fertilizer or something, some run off, and it was like that last year, but it'll clear up. He nods like he could make it happen, then glances over at the black ashes and charred trash, the leftovers of a recent burn. The scum stinks. Little bubbles of putrid gas trapped beneath the green slime. "Fuck," you say.

Later, in town, you see Les, but he's across the street and pretends not to see you. No sign of Holly although you watch for her. That you might see her, that she might show up holding the hand of a little girl, makes you nervous. What would you say?

You get a job at the plant bagging aluminum dross and iron oxide, making hot tops for the steel mills. During lunch you sit on a fifty-five-gallon drum of calcium oxide and eat a peanut butter sandwich, holding it in the wax paper because of the way the iron oxide embedded in your hands leaves dark red smudges on the bread. The men sitting around you say draft dodgers should be shot. They look to you for agreement even though none of them ever enlisted.

You stare at the clock on the wall, then toss your lunch bag at an empty barrel.

At home, you sit with your parents, watch The Carol Burnette show in color. Your parents laugh and laugh.

That the stains won't come out of your hands annoys you. The dark red oxide is in the pores, in the knuckles, in your eight fingers, and on the heel of your hands. No amount of washing or rubbing will get the red out. You walk toward the door and your parents want to know where you're going. "It's not over," your dad says. He looks at your mom, then at you and then back at the television.

You shrug, then head outside, go through the barn hunting for something, not a rake, not a shovel, something. You flip on the light and find an old window screen. That's one thing. And then you break a branch from the willow tree near the small creek and drag the branch and the screen along behind you to the scummed-over pond in the cuts. You kick off your shoes and wade into the green muck and start pushing it aside, using the screen as a sieve.

You throw the scum on the bank, then pull the willow branch across the water like a broom and move more scum into position and scoop it out. You do this over and over, throwing the smelly green algae up on the bank. You work for an hour, two. It's almost midnight, but the air is warm and damp. The green stuff is in your hair. It's stuck to your face, legs, and arms. You itch and smell.

But no matter how fast or hard you work, more scum floats into the small area you have cleared. Small clumps of it are everywhere and the odor is worse now than when you started. You toss the willow branch and screen aside. The soft, muddy bottom oozes between your toes. Water runs down your arms, drips off your elbows into the pond. A stone rolls down the steep side of the cut and plops into the water.

The quarter moon slowly sinking toward the horizon presses down against you. An oppressive weight. Cold. Lifeless. They've changed it. No doubt about it. The footprints and machinery are there. A conquered place.

Another quarter moon floats on the surface of the black water surrounded by drifting clouds of stinking algae. You look from one moon to the other, from the real to the illusion. One above and one below. It's late. You turn and walk away, squeezed between the two.

Uncle Easy

More than two-dozen mourners, including Easy's three former wives, took up the front pews of the country church, a church he had never attended. I sat next to my grandmother, who stared at her hands while my grandfather's milky eyes focused on the casket. The minister asked if anyone wanted to say a few words and heads turned, everyone waiting to see who would first step forward.

Easy's death—he was struck by lightning while fiddling with the antenna on the roof of his trailer—occurred on my grandparents' sixtieth wedding anniversary, and my father blamed his brother for choosing that day to die. "Couldn't even do that right," he said, adding this to his list of reasons for not attending the service.

"Anyone like to share a story about Ezekiel?" the minister repeated. "A fond memory?"

I took a deep breath and waited.

I was born seven months after Easy left for Vietnam, and the first time I could recall seeing him was at the funeral of my Aunt Irene. I was only six at the time and what I remembered was that he was tall with jet-black hair, had a hawk-like nose, and he looked uncomfortable in his white shirt and tie. We didn't speak, but he yanked my ponytail and gave a soft growl as he passed on his way to the casket.

Despite our frequent visits to my grandparents' farm and Easy living in a ramshackle trailer in the woods a short walk beyond the garden, I didn't see him again until five years later. As usual, my father pulled up to the sagging barn that cold, southern Ohio day and refused to turn off the engine of our rust-covered Studebaker. He gripped the steering wheel and slowly shook his head while I waited silently in the backseat, sandwiched between my brothers. The smell of manure drifted through the partially opened windows along with the fumes from the car's exhaust. My mother reached across the front seat and touched his arm. "Les?"

Dad's grip on the steering wheel tightened. "If he's here, we're going home."

He was Easy or Ezekiel, or E-Z, my father's brother. My mother called him Zeke.

"Everything will be fine," she said. "We can't leave without visiting your mom and dad." It was her standard answer to my father's standard threat.

My father turned off the engine, and my twin brothers, Bobby and Jeff, jumped out of the car and raced to the barn where they would build hay-bale forts. I was two years older than the twins, and the last time they made a fort I'd been the target of an attack that left me with hay down my back and a knot on my head. I ran past the two-seat outhouse, through the chicken yard, and up the hill.

The house, surrounded by abandoned strip mines, fields and woods, and originally a log cabin, had been sided with clapboard and topped with a tin roof, but inside the hand hewed beams were still visible. The two downstairs rooms straddled the crest of a hill, and over the years the house had settled so that the kitchen floor sloped downhill to the south while the living room, where the potbelly stove was located, sloped downhill to the north.

I opened the door and stepped into the kitchen. My uncle sat at the table, eyes half closed, blowing a cloud of cigarette smoke toward the ceiling.
I turned and looked for my father, but he and my mother had not yet arrived. My grandparents sat on the sofa in the other room watching a small television.

My father never said anything kind about his brother although my mother, when my father and brothers weren't around, occasionally dropped tags about my uncle, that he had been a promising pitcher, that he later lost two fingers and still had shrapnel in his back from Vietnam, that he'd been the wild one in the family. When she said *wild one*, she smiled.

"Anyone?" the minister asked again, a note of desperation in his voice.

My grandparents were quiet farmers and despite the minister's glances in their direction they remained glued to their seats with their heads down. My grandfather, who had the shakes and no teeth, nudged me with an elbow.

My parents and twin brothers did not attend the funeral. My father saw divorce as a sin against God, and his brother had been married and divorced two times, maybe three. (No one was sure if Zeke and Marvella had ever gotten hitched.) My father complained about Zeke's drinking and swearing and that he wore his baseball cap in the house. He resented his brother for being poor, which he felt reflected poorly on the entire family despite my parents being only marginally better off.

My brothers, who had both begun seminary school in Nashville, said they were sorry they couldn't attend, and they would pray for their uncle's soul. My mother came late and sat in the back pew, inconspicuous and alone.

The afternoon I encountered my uncle in my grandparent's kitchen, I didn't know which of his names I should call him. I took a step forward. "Uncle . . ."

He looked at me for a few seconds. "Easy," he said. My uncle squinted like he was about to unleash a fastball at a cleanup hitter's head.

"Uncle . . . Uncle Easy, I'm Lydia Wright."

"I know who you are," he said. "Get over here." He held out his hand, the three fingers splayed like a chicken's foot. "Put 'er there."

I took hesitant steps across the kitchen and reluctantly shook his hand. He had a strong grip, and he held me there while my heart pounded, and I wondered what would happen next. "Holly's girl."

"Yep." Apparently satisfied with my answer he released my hand and reached for a chipped cup next to his ashtray.

"Want some coffee?"

I'd never been asked if I wanted coffee, but before I could answer his eyes went from me to the door, and I knew my parents had stepped inside.

"Hello, Zeke," my mother said.

My uncle nodded. "Hello, Holly. Hello, Les."

I expected my father to turn and leave, tell me to get back to the car, but he ignored my uncle and stepped into the other room. My mother, maybe embarrassed by my father's behavior, stayed. "How you been? The farm treating you ok?" she asked.

My uncle grinned. "Ready for spring," he said, adding, "You're lookin' good." Then, after a moment of awkward silence and staring at me as if I was supposed to say something, my mother slipped away.

Uncle Easy cocked an eyebrow. "So, no coffee?" he asked.

"Not this time."

"Good," he said, "'cause the pot's empty. I'll make more in case you change your mind." He carried the coffee pot to the water bucket on the metal table by the backdoor and lifted the long-handled dipper with his three-fingered hand, but he lost his grip. The ladle fell to the bottom of the bucket.

"Shitgoddamnedsonofabitch," he said in a voice with more disbelief than anger.

I stepped back. I expected my father to charge around the corner and threaten his brother for what he'd said. He didn't tolerate swearing of any sort.

Dropping the dipper in the bucket was a mistake I'd once made. To get the dipper out you had to reach into the bucket, and no one wanted to drink the water after you'd dipped your hand in it. The only remedy was to empty the bucket in the backyard, a waste of water, and then pump fresh water into the bucket, an annoying process in good weather but especially irritating on a cold March day. The conversation in the other room stopped. My father stepped into the kitchen, glared at his brother. "You haven't changed," he said.

My father often warned my brothers if he ever heard them swear, they'd get their mouth washed out with soap. Being a girl, my father assumed I'd never swear, and I was spared the threat.

Uncle Easy had just said the S-word, the G.D.-word, and the S.O.B.-word in one breath.

"I'll fill the bucket," I said, hoping to escape before my father and uncle came to blows.

Easy stood up. "I'll keep you company," he said.

Being alone with him wasn't something I wanted. I stepped out the backdoor and onto the wet boards by the pump, my uncle close behind. A cold breeze whipped around the corner of the house. "Jesus H. Christ!" he said, clamping his hand onto his cap.

Whoops and hollers came from the barn. "Hey, Poop-eyes," my brothers yelled. "Come here!"

My uncle stopped and looked in the direction of the barn as if the insult had been directed at him. "Poop-eyes?"

"My brothers," I said. "I'm the only one in our family with brown eyes, and they want me to come to the barn, so they can throw hay down my back. I opened my eyes wide to show him.

My uncle spit in the mud next to the pump. "Someone talks to you like that don't answer. Understand? Nothing wrong with brown eyes." He leaned so close I could smell the cigarette smoke on his shirt as he pointed two of his three fingers at his own dark brown eyes.

"But there's two of them," I said.

"Shee-it."

"I'm a girl," I said, frustrated that he didn't see the obvious.

"Being a girl don't make you weak, and nothin' says you have to play fair when you're outnumbered."

The rebuke stung.

He clamped an unlit cigarette between his teeth. "Hold the damn bucket."

He primed the pump and water began to flow. The wire handle cut into my hand, but my uncle kept pumping.

Water lapped over the bucket's lip. Too late, I stepped back to avoid the water sloshing on my shoes. "It's full."

He gave the handle one more pump, then looked out at the woods beyond the barn. "We need warm rain for the mushrooms," he said.

"What mushrooms?" I asked.

"What mushrooms? You never hunt mushrooms?"

"No."

"Jesus H. Christ." He shook his head, shifted the cigarette to the corner of his mouth, and looked up at the clouds as if coming to an important decision. "I'll take you."

I didn't believe him. Adults were always saying they'd do something *someday* and then never doing it because they either forgot, something came up, or because they tried to get hold of you and you weren't home. That was okay with me. I didn't want to go mushroom hunting or anywhere else with my uncle, who might get drunk or violent or both. "Sure," I said.

I stepped inside where my father, car keys jangling in his hand, waited impatiently at the front door. "We're going," he said.

I hugged my grandparents and turned to say goodbye to my uncle, but he'd disappeared.

The congregation squirmed under the minister's gaze. A pretty, older woman with long black hair stood up and walked to the front of the church. "Zeke," she said without any preamble, "was the love of my life." She paused and looked at the minister with a smile that said, *You asked for this.* "And I know," she continued, "at least three other women who would say the same thing." There were chuckles behind us and my grandparents nodded their heads.

A month after the March encounter with my uncle, my grandmother called and asked if I could come to the farm for the weekend. She told my parents she hadn't had a chance to spend time with me on the previous visit, and she could use help planting the garden, adding the two boys might be too much for her. When my parents dropped me off Friday evening, my father warned me to avoid my uncle. "Don't go near him," he said.

What seemed like only a few hours after I fell asleep beneath a feather tick in the loft, the floorboards creaked. At first I thought it was one of my grandparents whose bed was on the other side of a moveable partition. A hand nudged my shoulder. "Get out of bed, girl!"

I bolted upright, unsure of the time or who was there. "What?" I asked.

"We're going mushroom huntin'."

It was still dark outside. Mushroom hunting? "Uncle . . .?"

"Easy. Call me Easy. Sweet Jesus! You forgot my name already? And I ain't gonna wait all day. See you downstairs."

I slipped from under the covers and, shivering in the cold loft, quickly dressed. My uncle sat at the table wearing a baseball cap and a stained, brown jacket. "There," he said, pointing at a plate with two slices of toast next to a cup of steaming coffee. "I'm guessing you like it black."

"Sure," I said, shocked by my answer. I ate the toast but could only swallow a few sips of the bitter, black coffee.

"Here," he said, handing me a paper bag. "Put it in your pocket."

"Isn't it a little early?" I was barely awake, the sun wasn't up, and I was supposed to help my grandmother plant her garden.

"Shit, no. We gotta get out before some sneaky son of a bitch follows us to our secret spot."

I nodded as if I understood. A few minutes later we walked down the path past the outhouse and climbed a fence. "Always climb at the post," he said. We passed his trailer—tottering on concrete blocks—and walked along the edge of deep, long cuts in the earth left from years of strip-mining coal. "I used to go swimming in that one," he said, pointing at a kidney shaped pond that was more mud than water. Eventually, we arrived at an oak and hickory woods. "Here," he said. "You know what they look like?"

I shook my head.

"A brown, spongy top on a light brown stalk." He held out two fingers on the three-fingered hand. "Yay big."

I stared at the ground as I followed my uncle back and forth through the trees. He picked up a stick. "Get one," he said, showing me how I could use the tip of the stick to turn over leaves or flip a snake out of the way.

He pointed at an umbrella-like plant. "Mayapples, good sign."

I swung my stick like a sword, taking off several umbrella tops and hoping to scare away anything that slithered or crawled.

"What you doin'?" he asked. "You want to tell everyone where we hunt?" He turned away, mumbling to himself.

Perhaps the few sips of coffee I'd had that morning sharpened my senses. His shocked expression at my whacking the Mayapples was almost funny. Just the same, I stopped swinging the stick. We walked forward three or four steps, paused, scanned the ground, and then continued forward. He motioned for me to move to the side. "No sense you looking at what I've already seen," he said.

We came to an area where the ground was damp, the soil black, and he signaled for me to stop. "Looky there."

I looked.

"There," he said, pointing his stick at the ground in front of my feet.

I looked again and, as if by magic, where I'd seen nothing before, I now saw a spongy, dark brown top on a light brown stalk. I stepped forward to pick it.

"Stop! Jesus! Look first," he said.

I studied the ground around my feet and saw a dozen mushrooms, maybe more. Carefully, I knelt down.

"Don't go yanking those outta the ground. Here, use this."
He handed me a pearl-handled pocketknife, and I cut the mushrooms at the bottom of the stalks.
"There you go. Now put them in your bag and hang onto the knife."

He smoked a cigarette down to the butt, shredded what was left, rolled up the paper, and stuck it in his pocket. He caught me watching. "Field dressing," he said. "Don't ever start smokin'. Hear? It's a dirty habit."

The shadows grew shorter and the day warmer as we continued our search. My uncle swore when he didn't find any mushrooms and swore when he did.

After we filled our bags, we left the woods and began to head back.

I held out the pocketknife he'd loaned me. "Thanks."

"Keep it," he said. "And don't let it rust. Hear?"

I nodded. My brothers had pocketknives. I had scissors. My father would've been furious if he knew I got a knife from Uncle Easy.

"You sure?" I asked.

"I'm sure," he said.

I slipped it into my pocket where it tapped against my leg, a reminder this day would be a secret.

Our route back to the trailer was a big arc meant to deceive anyone watching for clues as to where we'd been. We were crossing a gravel road when a black Chevy stopped, and the driver, a man with big ears and slicked back hair, a man about my uncle's age, asked what I had in my bag. I held up a large mushroom.

"Give you two bucks for the poke," he said.

My uncle stepped between me and the car.

"Five bucks," the guy said, taking out his wallet and waving the money at me.

Five bucks was a lot of money, and my father once said his brother didn't have two dimes to rub together.

Easy ripped the five out of the guy's hand. "Go, you greedy son of a bitch. Git!"

"Give me the bag or give back my money," the guy said, his head sticking out the open window.

"Come and take it, you son of a bitch."

I was scared. I thought someone was going to get killed.

The driver hesitated and Uncle Easy took a step toward the car, grabbed the antenna and broke it off. "You're crazy, Zeke," the driver yelled as the car took off, spitting gravel as it raced down the road.

"Thinks he can buy everything," Easy said as we climbed the fence on the other side of the road. "Here, want an antenna?"

I shook my head, and he flipped the antenna in the ditch.

I worried the guy might come for us. I kept thinking, *Get back to my grandparents. Get back to the farm.* "You know him?" I asked.

"Carl Wood. Married Marvella."

Marvella? I cleared my throat. "Wasn't she your wife?"

Easy tucked the five-dollar bill into his pocket as we followed a cow path through a pasture. "Marvella," he said. "We kept each other warm."

I didn't ask although I had an idea.

When we arrived at my uncle's trailer, I held out my bag of mushrooms. "Thanks for taking me," I said. "It was fun."

"Fun? Jesus! What's wrong with you? Best part is the eatin'."

I didn't know what to say. The mushrooms were ugly, maybe poisonous, and the trailer was dented and leaning like a sinking ship.

The door groaned as he swung it open. "Wipe your feet," he said.
I followed him inside.

The trailer's interior was dark with only the outline of a lamp and a chair visible until he pulled back a faded blue towel that served as a curtain. A small table covered with tubes, wires, and other parts of a radio sat against the wall, and engine parts I didn't recognize filled a wood crate on the floor. A chair by the window had lost most of its stuffing. Wire-rimmed glasses rested on a stack of

Field and Stream magazines.

We soaked the mushrooms in saltwater, cut them in half—they were hollow—and shook them inside a bag of flour. He pointed at the refrigerator, told me to get the butter, which I found on a plate between brown beer bottles and blue coffee cans. After he had the mushrooms simmering in the skillet to his satisfaction, he turned the job over to me while he brewed coffee in a badly dented pot. The fried mushrooms piled up on a plate.

"You like it black, right?" he asked. The coffee perked on the stove.

"Right," I lied, wondering if I had a choice.

"Go ahead," he said, shoving the plate of mushrooms toward me.

"Aren't some poisonous?" I asked.

He grinned. "The wrong ones 'll kill ya."

I picked the smallest one I could find. They no longer looked disgusting, and I took a nibble while my uncle watched.

"Yeah?" he said.

It was good, a little like the coating on fried chicken but much better. I ate the rest of it, then picked up a bigger one and ate that one, too. He nodded approval, swept the radio parts to the side with his forearm and put the plate between us on the table. He dropped a loaf of bread next to the plate and inspected a slice for mold. "I like to make mushroom sandwiches," he said.

I made a mushroom sandwich, too.

He pointed at the stove, told me to pour myself a cup of coffee.

I wanted to ask about his missing fingers, what happened to him and Marvella, and why there was bad blood between him and my father. Instead, I held the coffee cup between my hands the way he held his and surveyed the small room, the feed mill calendar by the window, a mouse scurrying along the wall and disappearing down a hole in the floor.

He caught me eyeing the fishing pole in the corner. "You fish?" he asked.

"No."

"Then we'll go fishing this fall," he said. "I'll show you how to catch the big ones."

My mind had wandered. The woman, I guessed she might be Marvella, sat down and the minister, apparently pleased someone had stepped forward, asked if anyone else would say a few words. A former classmate of Easy's stood up, went to the altar and told a story about the time Easy was baling hay and stopped the tractor near the fencerow to give a milk snake time to slither out of the way. "He loved animals," the man said. "After he got back from Vietnam, he refused to hunt."

I kept my pocketknife and my relationship with Easy a secret. The twins never asked about my weekend, and, as my uncle advised, I stood up to them, kneeing them each in the groin until they stopped pinching and bullying me. I was changing, and my parents didn't know what to make of it.

Every time we returned to my grandparents' farm, my father made his usual threat about leaving if he saw his brother. While my brothers swung on ropes in the hayloft and shot at blackbirds with their homemade slingshots, I sneaked down the lane and visited my uncle who welcomed me by pointing at the coffee pot and telling me to help myself. Then, after my cup was half empty, we'd move to a table where he was repairing a radio, or we'd step outside where he was welding a broken wheel for a hay wagon. Once, we went for a long walk through the fields, so he could show me a hen quail and her eight chicks, which were, he said, "as cute as tits on a turtle."

In October of that first year of knowing Easy, just as the leaves were beginning to turn, my parents dropped me off at the farm to help my grandmother with her canning. Early the following morning a hand shook my shoulder. "Get out of bed, girl," my uncle said. "God, how late do you sleep?"

The sun was not yet up.

A half hour later we were hiking through a field heavy with dew. My uncle carried a canvas bag and a small tackle box. I carried two fishing poles. We climbed fences, tightrope-walked a log across the creek, and, after circling the stripper cuts, arrived at a long, narrow pond.

"Think it's safe to fish here?" I asked, pointing the tip of the poles at the NO TRESPASSING! sign.

My uncle winked at me and opened the tackle box. A few minutes later he was pointing at the water. "Your bobber! Yank!" he said.

There was no bobber. A fish had pulled it under. I flipped the tip of the pole the way he showed me and soon landed my first fish.

"Nice bass," he said.

I was putting a fresh night crawler on my hook when I heard a tractor chugging toward us, an old guy on the seat yelling and waving a shotgun. My uncle motioned for me to cast my line back in the water.

"And stop slouching," he said. "We're not hiding."

The tractor stopped, the old farmer climbed off, cradling the shotgun in his arms like a baby. "Zeke? Should have known it was you. Can't you read?"

Uncle Easy looked at the NO TRESPASSING sign. "We're not smoking," he said, winking at me and grinning.

The farmer looked from my uncle to me and back to my uncle. "You're crazy, Zeke," he said. "And leave some for me!" Then he left.

One second I thought we were going to be shot or thrown in jail and the next I was tossing my line back in the water. "He's high strung," my uncle said by way of an explanation. "He owes me. I repaired his baler."

We ate peanut butter sandwiches my grandmother had made and drank coffee from a thermos in my uncle's canvas pack. After lunch we took a break and made sketches of the cattails and the dragonflies that hugged them. By afternoon the stringer was full of fish.

Aunt Viola, my father's younger sister, dressed in black except for her white nursing shoes, walked up to the altar, glanced at me, and began. "Zeke was a kind man," she said, looking at me again as if I might be a proxy for my father. "Before he left for Vietnam every woman this side of Unity wanted to be his girlfriend and every guy wanted to be his best buddy. He was full of life and fun to be around. He was like a young boy wrapped in a man's body. If only the backseat of his old Chevy could talk. Whew!"

The minister blushed and forced a smile.

My uncle and I continued to go mushroom hunting every spring and fishing every fall. He taught me how to play poker one winter and kept the two bucks I lost. Together, we repaired radios, stacked wood, and planted a small flower garden next to the trailer. He liked zinnias. Over the next four years I grew eight inches, passing both brothers and my parents in height. I was nearly as tall as my uncle. Easy helped me with my science project, a radio telescope, and encouraged me to stand up for myself and to not to take shit from anyone. When I was seventeen, I took Carl my first real boyfriend, to the farm. Easy thawed three frozen Hostess cupcakes in the oven to celebrate the occasion.

Carl thought I had my uncle's dark brown eyes, and when my grandmother said I had Easy's smirk down pat, I was pleased.

My aunt, now that she had started telling stories about her brother, was reluctant to stop. "Here's another thing," she said, pausing to look at me again. "Zeke lost two fingers and was badly wounded in Vietnam. Got the Purple Heart and Distinguished Service Cross." She nodded for emphasis.

I'd seen the medals along with a rifle casing and a pair of sergeant stripes while rummaging through coffee cans looking for a stick of charcoal. When I held them up to ask, my uncle shook his head. He didn't talk about the past. He never mentioned my father although he often told me to be good to my mother. Sometimes, when we were fishing or at the table playing cards or repairing a radio, I'd catch him watching me. He'd nod and I'd nod back.

"Anyone else?" the minister asked after my aunt took her seat.

I imagined Easy telling me to get off my ass. I tugged at the neck of my sweater and stood up. The minister nodded. I walked to the front of the church, stood straight, shoulders back. No slouching. My mother, sitting in the shadows, was barely visible. "Easy," I said, pausing to organize my thoughts, what I could say and what I wouldn't, "taught me to fish, hunt mushrooms, play poker, and stand straight. I'm here today because of him."

ENTANGLEMENT

Shards

Lydia:

My father and I had returned from a shopping trip at Eastland Mall, and I was in the kitchen looking for something to eat when he howled. I ran to the bedroom to see what was wrong. He tried to hold me back, but I saw her. I couldn't scream. I couldn't breathe.

"Get outside," he said. "Get in the car and lock the doors."

There was blood everywhere, on the floor, the walls, the bed, the door.

"Go!" he yelled.

I ran to the car and locked myself in. I was terrified. There were sirens, flashing lights, a policeman knocking on the window, asking if I was okay.

I was shuttled to my grandparents. "What happened? What happened?" I kept asking, but no one explained. I cried so hard I couldn't catch my breath. The next day *The Daily Leader* ran a front-page article that raised more questions and provided no answers.

Hennesey, the last person to see his wife alive, told his daughter to remain in the car when the family returned from eating lunch at a local restaurant. He entered the house with his wife, reappeared minutes later, alone, and then drove to the mall, a shopping trip in which nothing was bought. According to Hennesey, he discovered his wife's body when he and his daughter returned home.

My grandmother, my mom's mom, studied the newspaper article, clucking her tongue while filing the clipping in a red folder. This all happened on the north side of Columbus, Ohio. Flippo the clown lived on our street, which isn't important except to say you'd've never expected a murder on the street where a famous clown lived. In the middle of the day? I jumped every time the phone rang, expecting my mother to call and apologize for the confusion. I had nightmares. The leaves had turned and were falling in the backyard. That seemed important. I don't know why.

I worried where I'd live if my father went to prison. I didn't think he was guilty, but why did the police and my grandparents treat him like he was?

Three days after it happened, the police interviewed me. Detectives. They looked like car salesmen and wore white shirts and flashy ties, not police uniforms. We sat at a cafeteria-like table in a room with windows but no pictures on the walls. Fluorescent lights buzzed overhead. One detective nodded. The other leaned forward and said what he could to make me comfortable. Not good cop, bad cop. Talker and nodder.

The talker tapped his pen on the table. Tap, tap, tap until he caught me staring. "Oh, sorry," he said. "I quit smoking and . . ."
I thought he was Italian. His last name gave me that impression.

The woman sitting next to me squirmed in her chair and jangled the five hundred silver bracelets on her wrist. She smelled like the cosmetic counter at Lazarus. She was supposedly there to protect me although I didn't know what she was supposed to protect me from. She smiled and patted my arm. I didn't like being touched by strangers.

The talker said they were sorry about my mom. He waited a few seconds and then asked how I was doing.

I missed my mother, couldn't sleep, had these sharp pains in my chest and stomach, and hated staying with my grandmother. She coddled me like I was a baby, and then she cried. My grandfather didn't say squat. He looked at me, ran a hand over his face, shook his head and walked away. My uncle Denny, despite being warned not to ask questions, stopped over and wanted to know what happened, if I saw her body, if I knew who did it, was I scared. I said I wasn't scared but I was. I wanted to go home, back to my house, but that wasn't possible.

"Okay," I said to the detective. "I'm okay."

Eventually, he got around to the questions he wanted to ask.

"Lydia, the three of you—you, your mom, and your dad—went out for lunch that day, right?"

Before I could answer the quiet one, the nodder, asked, "You remember where you went, Lydia?"

"Perkins."

The nodder nodded like I'd given the correct answer. The talker said he was a big fan of Perkins. They were treating me like my grandmother.

"You remember what the three of you talked about, Lydia?"

I tried to remember. The woman with the jangling bracelets and smelling of perfume and powder patted my wrist again. I wanted to open one of the windows. I needed air. "Our pancakes, I guess."

"So, the three of you had pancakes, Lydia?"

They were driving me nuts. Lydia, Lydia, Lydia. They didn't have to repeat my name every time they asked a question, and I couldn't imagine why they asked if we had pancakes. What did that have to do with my mother's murder? "No, just my dad and me. Mom said she had to watch her weight and ordered . . ." I couldn't remember what she had, and I started crying. I mean I was out of control. Sobbing, choking, bottom lip quivering, tears running down my cheeks and falling on the table. I was a mess.

The woman pushed a box of tissues in my direction and signaled for them to give me a break, which they did, bringing me a vending machine Baby Ruth. I whispered to the woman to tell them to stop repeating my name.

They looked embarrassed, and I thought maybe they'd never done this before. For some reason that made me feel better.

"Your parents argue about anything? Anything at all?" The talker asked.

My father had said he wanted to run to the mall and my mother said she wanted to get home. I didn't know how it became an argument. "No," I said.

"They didn't argue."

They didn't believe me.

The Italian-looking one, the talker—I can't remember his name—read the questions from notes he had in front of him. "So, when your father took your mother home, did you go inside with them or wait in the car?"

I felt guilty, like if I'd gone inside my father would have an alibi. "I waited."

"Did your father tell you to wait?"

"My father had to go to the bathroom. I didn't."

"Your father went inside?"

"He couldn't pee outside on the bushes!" I was repeating what I'd heard my uncle say this to my grandmother.

I crumpled my candy wrapper and looked for a wastebasket but didn't see one. Outside, a girl walking a small dog passed on the sidewalk. I wanted to be that girl, walking with a dog of my own, away from the questions.

They asked how long my father was in the house. I didn't know.

"Was your father upset when he came out? Had he changed clothes?"

I didn't remember but said, no and no.

Talker looked at his notes. "Did your mother step out and wave goodbye before you left?"

My lip started to quiver. "No."

A week later, after we were back in our house, the police showed up and took my father away in the cruiser. "Just a few more questions," they said. Across the street, Mrs. Horton pulled back the curtains and watched. The next day my father hired a lawyer. My grandmother thought this made him look guilty.

The following spring my father started seeing Judy, a bottle blond who worked at an insurance office. She talked to me like the detectives. Do you like school? What's your favorite subject? On and on. She wanted to be my mother. It wasn't going to happen.

My father seeing someone so soon after the murder encouraged more gossip. My grandmother and Denny asked how I felt about my dad and Judy. I didn't answer, which was answer enough I suppose.

Even after the walls were painted and new carpet installed my father kept the bedroom door locked. The neighbors continued to talk. People we didn't know stopped in front of our house and pointed. Some turned in our drive and sat for a moment before moving on. Eventually, my father said it was time to start over. He and Judy found a house in a small town south of Columbus and we moved.

Tina:

I was talking on the phone with Doreen and saw them pull up, four cruisers with flashing lights. Doreen and I were best friends and about to start high school. "I have to go," I said, hanging up and running to the front door before the cops knocked. Cops had been to our house before. Usually there were two and usually they talked with my dad outside in the garage where he worked on his motorcycle. This time they had a posse. Cops at the front door, cops walking around the side of our house, cops standing by the cruisers. I wondered how I'd describe it when my mother got home.

A cop so big he filled the doorway looked down at me. No smile. No frown. "Your father here?" He had the sad eyes of a bulldog and a voice so deep it vibrated my ribs.

"Maybe," I said, wishing I'd warned my dad before opening the door.

'Tina," he said.

His knowing my name threw me off. I pointed at the backroom.

More cops followed him inside. I couldn't see if their guns were drawn because the giant herded me into the kitchen and blocked my view. I thought he would be the one to go to my father, but no, big cop with me, small cops went for my father. Go figure.

Dad's arms and shoulders bulged with muscles and tattoos. He rode with the Chosen Few and had a swagger like Stone Cold Steve Austin crossing the ring. When I was little I thought riding in the motorcycle gang was his job. Some of my classmates, the ones who met my father, were afraid of me because of the way he looked. The cops didn't look afraid.

"You alone?" the giant asked, blocking my escape from the kitchen.

"Why do you want my father?"

"Are you alone, Tina?" he repeated. "Is your mother home?"

"Answer my question and I'll answer yours," I said.

He turned and looked toward the living room like he thought someone might be sneaking up on him. "We need to talk with your dad about something important."

I took in the kitchen, the dirty dishes in the sink, the empty beer bottles on the counter, and the pile of newspapers on the table, some stained with the oil my father used to clean his gun. It was close to suppertime and my mother had told me to clean up before she got home. I was going to catch shit.

A woman cop entered the kitchen. She didn't look old enough or strong enough to be a cop, but there she was, rosy cheeks and perfect teeth, hand resting on the butt of her gun. Just showing off. "No one else here," she said. She gave me a look, half pity, half why hadn't I cleaned up the mess in the kitchen. "Your mom at work?" she asked.

For a minute I thought they were going to arrest me. "Yes," I said.

She picked up the phone, punched in the number listed on the card hanging on the wall, asked for my mother, and told her she needed to come home right away.

The giant paced around the kitchen, stopped at my sketch of Fast Eddie, one of Dad's friends, racing down a highway on his Harley. "You do this?" he asked, lifting his chin at the drawing taped to the side of the refrigerator. He leaned in closer. "You're good."

I moved toward the doorway to see what was going on with my dad.

"Stay here," he said. "Take a seat."

I pushed the pile of newspapers aside, covering the gun oil stains, and pulled out a chair.

"Can we get you anything?" the woman asked.

I wanted to say it was my home and if I wanted anything I could damn well get it myself. I said, "No."

They took in the dirty dishes piled in the sink, the spaghetti stain on the side of the wastebasket, the hunting magazines scattered on the counter, trying to be casual about it as if they weren't really looking. I wasn't fooled.

My father called from the living room as the cops led him handcuffed to the front door. "Tina, tell your mother it's a mix up," he said.

There'd been a lot of mix-ups.

When he drove a semi delivering new Chevy Impalas from Lordstown to dealers in central Ohio, he was caught stripping radios and spare tires out of the cars. He was fired and got a job at a sports store. That lasted until he came under suspicion for selling guns illegally outside of work. Twice, he was charged with assault. The first time charges were dropped when the guy refused to testify. The second time he did six months in county.

During hunting season he pretended to be a game warden. When he caught a guy hunting without a license, he'd take his gun, which the guy could supposedly retrieve after paying a fine. Of course, no one ever got their gun back or could find the game warden who had stopped them in the fields. A silver-plated .45 automatic was his favorite, and he'd sit at the kitchen table, taking it apart, oiling it, and then putting it back together. He liked hunting knives, too.

He was gone a lot, often disappearing for a week or longer. If Mom knew where he was she never said, and I learned not to ask. Sometimes his absences were welcomed. He had a temper, especially when he was drinking, and had punched holes in the bedroom wall, but he could whistle better than anyone. I wanted him to go on *Star Search*. Money problems solved. He could be good in other ways, too. He took me for a ride on his bike a few times. And on a hot night the previous summer our neighbor across the street, Cliff Davis, stood in his front yard with a shotgun and threatened to kill his wife. Dad got him calmed down, and by the time the cops came the neighborhood was quiet, like nothing had happened.

Grass didn't grow in our front yards and most of the houses needed paint, but other than the night Cliff Davis waved the shotgun there weren't many problems. My dad convinced the driver of the ice cream truck to go down our street on Saturdays, and, if I was fast enough to catch him, he'd give me a cone. No charge. Make mine chocolate, thanks. I often left my bike in the front yard, and it was never stolen.

Sitting at the table, staring out the window, waiting for my mother, I imagined the whole neighborhood buzzed with curiosity.

"Have you eaten?" the woman cop asked. Pink lipstick and red hair. What was she thinking? She glanced around the kitchen like a large pepperoni pizza might suddenly appear.

"No," I said, and then, as if she was reading my mind, she picked up the phone, called Pizza Hut, and ordered a large pepperoni pizza. I don't know how that happened.

Mom arrived at the same time as the pizza. Pink lipstick/red hair paid.

"What's he done this time?" Those were my mother's first words when she saw the cops.

The giant and the skinny redhead exchanged a glance. "He's being questioned," the giant said. Which didn't tell us anything.

"He'll never learn," Mom said. She looked at the pizza box. "You staying?"

I could see they'd expected her to go after them, make a big fuss, but instead she said they could stay and have pizza since they paid for it. I wondered if she was trying to get on their good side to help my father out of his situation whatever it was.

They didn't stay although I wished they had because with them around my mother might not have lit into me over not cleaning up the kitchen.

The next day Fast Eddie, came around to find out what was what. Before he left he saw the drawing I'd made of him and peeled off a fifty for it. I shook off the money. "You don't have to buy it," I said.

"Do not give your art away," he said. "Hear? Some day you'll be famous and this drawing will be worth thousands."

I didn't believe him but I took the fifty.

The next day we learned my father had been charged with murder. The murder had happened three years earlier in a rich neighborhood north of Columbus. People were getting murdered all the time. I had no idea which murder he was supposed to have done. I couldn't imagine a murder on the north side having anything to do with him.

Three more of Dad's motorcycle buddies showed up and talked with my mother. They wanted to buy a few of Dad's things, things he had stored in the garage. They never said what the things were, but I could have guessed. My mother told them to help themselves. They handed her an envelope stuffed with cash and said if we ever needed anything to let them know. She told me to forget the whole thing. I didn't.

I hoped Fast Eddie would come back. He didn't

The story was in the newspaper. According to the front-page article, when Dad was in jail for the assault charge, he told his cellmate one of his robberies had gone bad. He'd stabbed a woman who surprised him. Why he told the guy, I don't know. Maybe time in jail gets boring and his story was a chance to liven things up. Maybe, and I often think this was the case, his cellmate had committed a major crime and my father, never one to be outdone, thought telling this guy he'd murdered a woman would give him more jailhouse cred. Unfortunately for my father, his cellmate was later charged with GTA—that's grand theft auto to the uninformed—and, remembering the conversation with my father, realized he had a bargaining chip.

My mother freaked out. She said how could you believe a snitch, one that supposedly remembered an old conversation. She was angry. I was angry, too, at my father, at the cops, at the snitch, and even at the woman who had been murdered. What had she done that provoked my father to kill her? Eventually, my mother started talking about my father running around with Blaze during the time of the murder. "Remember him?" she asked. "Blaze with the skull tat on his forehead?"

"The one you told me to stay away from?"

"Yeah, yeah," she said. "I can see your dad doing something crazy with him."

I didn't know what to think. Then, knowing he wouldn't be coming home, I was secretly relieved.

My mother visited him a couple times. I went with her once. The prison: colorless concrete blocks, stern-faced guards, sounds, and voices bouncing around like the place was hollow. My father didn't act angry, but he wouldn't whistle when I asked. Afterward, my mother said it was no place for a young girl. I didn't think it was a place for an older girl either. I didn't go back.

The prosecutors gave my father a choice: confess and get sentenced for life without parole or go before a jury and take a chance on getting the chair. He confessed.

We got phone calls, suspicious looks every time we went shopping at Kroger. Even the bald guy on the other side of the deli counter eyed us like we were murderers. We got an unlisted phone number, but that wasn't enough. I was no longer welcome at after school get-togethers. Even Doreen's mother worried about me coming around. My teachers eyed me like killing might run in the family. Eventually, my mother changed our last name and we moved in with my aunt, Mom's sister, who lived near a small town south of Columbus.

Lydia:

Our new house was old, like a hundred years old. Dad and Judy called it charming. They said it had character. At night the floors creaked and the walls popped like it was haunted. So yeah, it had character, a ghost. I wasn't happy my father married Judy, and I missed my friends. I missed my mother. Then, shortly after our boxes were unpacked and the curtains hung, Judy had a baby, a crying, screaming baby boy. Dad and Judy had been "dating" for six months. You do the math. What with the house popping and the baby crying I couldn't sleep.

My father sued the northside police department and the newspaper, claiming they smeared his name and led people to believe he murdered his wife. Judy talked constantly about what they could do with the settlement when they won their case, their case like it had anything to do with her. Go to Aruba. Go to Hawaii. Go on a cruise. Her dream trips never included me, and no matter how much I begged for a dog we couldn't get one because Judy had allergies.

I was in the ninth grade when they arrested the man who murdered my mother. That brought back the nightmares, the sharp pains in my stomach and chest. Judy said I had issues and complained they'd never escape the past.

A few months later, my uncle Denny, who kept track of things, told us the killer's wife and daughter had changed their last name and moved to our town. Soon after, this skinny bitch with a scowl, swinging hips, a chip on her shoulder, and jeans so tight you could've seen the year on the dime in her pocket sashayed into Mr. Oakley's English classroom like she owned the place. I knew who she was because my uncle had warned us and because she looked like a killer's kid.

So, when it was my turn to introduce myself, I said my last name and then my full name—you know, like, "Bond, James Bond." The new girl got an I-don't–believe-this-shit look, turned, and stared out the window where there was nothing to see except a parking lot and a football field full of dandelions.

She knew I knew, but we both pretended we didn't.

Tina:

The Plains! Whoever heard of a town called The Plains, not Plains, The Plains. Look it up. I knew we were fucked as soon as we got off Route 33 and I saw the sign. Call it ESP or whatever. A one-traffic light town in the middle of nowhere. Honest to God, I didn't know places like this existed. My father's motorcycle buddies would've loved it.

My aunt lived in a mobile home between Pickett's Gunworks and the Zion Church, next to railroad tracks that went who knew where. We were surrounded by trees, hills, and giant rocks. There might even have been bears in the woods for all I knew. The mobile home was so small I had to go outside to change my mind.

First day at school the guidance counselor hemmed and hawed while he tried to figure out what classes to put me in. "Well," he said, scratching his chin and then pushing his glasses higher on his nose. "Well." He disappeared to another office and was gone fifteen minutes. I ate the candy in the bowl on his desk, peppermint puffs and Tootsie Rolls. My mother didn't understand why I was so thin. I stashed the suckers in my backpack. Never know when you're going to get hungry.

After the counselor returned and looked at his empty candy bowl, he handed me my schedule, and I went to class where right off I was assigned a seat next to a too-pretty girl who eyed me up and down, taking inventory. "This is Tina," he said to the class. He asked everyone to introduce themselves, which might have been okay in the first grade, but this was tenth grade for Christ sakes. Anyway, when the introductions came to the too-pretty girl she said her name— first and last. I thought, fuck me. Of all the places on the planet, I was stuck sitting next to the girl whose mother my father killed.

What? Was I supposed to apologize? You can't make this shit up.

I was ready to take off, run away, hitchhike to California, get as far away as possible. The one thing that kept me from jumping out the English classroom window—it was ground level and opened wide enough so that a jump would have been easy—was the look. She glared at me. Hate and contempt, all wrapped up in that pretty little face. That's when I knew she knew. I gave her a blank stare, which is something I'd mastered with my father's friend Falco when he'd say something inappropriate, which was every time he opened his lipless mouth. Asshole. Anyway, right then I knew I couldn't run away. I couldn't let her think she scared me off. Know what I mean?

I thought it might be our secret, but within a week it was obvious the teachers knew. They went out of their way to make sure we didn't work together in art, biology, history, or phys. ed. We were always assigned separate groups or teams. Eventually our classmates knew, too. They gave me space.

It went on like this for three fucking years! We never said a word to each other, not one. Locker assignments were made alphabetically, so we should've been next to each other, but Lydia's locker was at one end of the hall and mine was at the other. She was in the cool rich kid crowd, the pretty-girl-cheerleader-jock group. I wasn't in a group and had no friends other than Toni Ferris, who shared cigarettes with me in the girl's lav.

My aunt and I went for long hikes in the hills. She knew all the wildflowers. Trillium, bluebells, phlox. I sketched and painted them. I was into watercolors.

Lydia:

Nothing made Judy happy, not even the money from the settlement. She grimaced when my grandmother or uncle would say how much I looked like my mother. She complained about me being out late and running around. She didn't like the clothes I wore. "Too provocative," she said. This coming from a woman who wore miniskirts and halter tops when she was dating my father. And she expected me to babysit every time she and my dad went golfing at the country club. They argued. Judy complained about the kitchen drawer missing knives. My father said I'd lost my mother, was working through it and needed counseling.

So.

I had this session with call-me-Father-Mike who was old as dirt and more interested in warning me about the "sins of the flesh" than how to cope with a crazy stepmother and a killer's daughter.

I got pregnant my senior year. So much for sins of the flesh. I lost the baby and then got pregnant again a year after graduation. I was fertile. You had to give me that. I had the baby the second time although Lucas, the baby's father, took his red hair and big teeth to the army before he could take on responsibilities. I named the baby Abby after my mother, which should have pleased my father, but Judy complained. That woman will always be hanging over us! After Abby came I was tired and depressed as hell. Sometimes a drink or a joint helped. Sometimes I thought about stabbing myself. "How much do I look like my mother now?" I'd've asked.

I moved in with a guy who had the same first name as my mother's killer. Maybe that was why it didn't work out.

Tina:

Because we never talked to each other didn't mean we didn't know what was what. Lydia got caught snorting a line in the Methodist Church parking lot. No jail time. I don't know how that happened.

My senior year I got a job at The Gentleman's Club just off the main highway south of Lancaster. I lied about my age and had a fake ID. And no, I didn't do drugs and I didn't do sex. I danced. One night I had over a hundred bucks stuffed in my G-string. Money coming out my kazoo. Literally. Gus, the guy who ran the place, said I was a natural.

After high school I began taking courses at Hocking Technical College. Art and Design. One evening I was grabbing something to eat in the student union before heading to the Club when this cop stopped me. I didn't want to talk with him. We had history, and I was moving on. He insisted I have a seat next to him, so I did.

"Eric died," he said.

Eric was his son. I'd only known Eric for a few hours one afternoon when he was dying of brain cancer. I liked him, and the news of his death hit me harder than I would've expected.

I was supposed to be at the Club, and I was running late.
The cop ran his fingers through his hair. "I don't know what to do," he said. "I should have done more for him, spent more time with him." He shivered like a dog throwing water off his coat. "Sorry," he added, taking off his hat and sweeping his hand through his hair. "Just thought . . ."

It was like an alarm going off, telling me time might be shorter than I thought. We sat and talked for an hour, maybe more, trying to bridge that loneliness we each felt.

Weirdly, his visit made me think about my life and what I wanted to do with it in the time I had. Every night the same stupid music, the sore feet, fingernails scratching my skin as some fat, drooling putz tried to jam a buck in my g-string. The novelty had worn off. I wanted to spend more time in the studio at school. I never showed up at the club that night or ever again. So it goes. Crazy. I celebrated my freedom and soon-to-be poverty with a chocolate milkshake at the Sonic Drive-in outside Nelsonville.

Then, another death. My father died in prison of a heart attack. For years he'd been like a ghost to me, lurking in shadows, in the sound of a Harley roaring down the road, or the whistling of a stranger. And then he became one, a ghost. Five years later, I opened The Glass Menagerie, a ceramic and stained-glass studio, with Ken, my partner. Lydia came into our gallery once, a Saturday morning in the spring, the day before Mother's Day. We recognized each other after a few seconds although we'd both changed. She looked as if the blood had been sucked out of her, and my first thought was she was there to ask for money, not to buy anything. She walked around the studio, picking up one piece, looking at the price, putting it back on the shelf, and then looking at another. I wanted to ask if she was okay, if I could help her find something. "Lydia?" I said. "Care for a cup of coffee?"

She turned and walked toward the door, but before leaving she picked up a hand-blown ruby red vase I'd blown a week earlier. I thought she was going to steal it or, hopefully, carry it to the counter and pull out her credit card. Instead, she held it at arm's length, gave me that tenth grade look of hate and contempt, stepped outside, and dropped it on the sidewalk where it shattered in a thousand sharp, red pieces.

Like Flying

Carl and Janet sat on a bench across from Cosmic Ray's Starlight Café, waiting for Eric, who was in Tomorrowland with a girl he'd met while standing in line. Carl was pleased Eric was having fun but knew Janet resented him being off with the girl instead of with them. Maybe worried was a better word. Still, Carl hoped they could take advantage of their time alone to talk.

Eric and the girl had been standing close to each other when a man with yellow boxer shorts sticking out the top of his jeans walked by humming the "Battle Hymn of the Republic." That's how it started, the two of them snickering. Later, she asked Eric if he was coming back over spring break, his baldness and six-foot three frame fooling her into thinking he was older than he was. Carl had held his breath as he waited for Eric's answer, then for her reaction, but Eric only said, no, he wouldn't be back. She'd said her name, but Carl couldn't remember it. Loreena, Lauren, maybe Laura. She wore bright pink shorts with lettering across the seat, and Carl had caught himself staring, trying to make out the word.

The rides were off limits for Eric except those suitable for the very young and the very old, and he had been pleased to find someone close to his own age in line for Stitch's Great Escape. As they moved forward, he turned to his parents and suggested they meet later, say at Cosmic Ray's. Say around six.

But now he was ten minutes late and nowhere in sight. "He'll be here in a minute," Carl said.

Janet sat with her arms across her chest and stared at a Japanese couple with a young boy coming out of Auntie Gravity's Galactic Goodies. Carl was about to say that Eric had just lost track of time when she turned and said, "He's fifteen minutes late. I don't know why we agreed to this."

Carl wanted to say that Eric was sixteen, and, all things considered, he ought to be doing what he wanted. Carl suspected Eric had come on the trip to Disney World not for himself, but for them, especially his mother who had planned it. His one stipulation had been that there were to be no pictures. The camera had to be left at home.

Carl looked at his watch. He was hungry. "Want an ice cream cone?" he asked. He worried that Janet might give him that look, the one that accused him of not feeling the pain as deeply as she did.

"Something could be wrong," she said. "What if something happened? This was stupid."

By *this*, Carl assumed she meant leaving Eric. Disneyworld had been her idea. She wanted Eric to have experiences, but Carl thought they were wearing Eric out, making time pass too quickly. The three of them could have been at an IHOP downing a stack of blueberry pancakes or fishing with Eric's granddad. He glanced over at the Plaza Ice Cream Parlor. He sensed Janet resented that he could still get hungry when Eric was off with the girl, but she nodded. "Vanilla," she said.

Secretly, he was proud of Eric, the way he had chatted with the girl, teasing her about her oversized box of popcorn until she poured some into his hand. Carl had never been much of a talker. Words tumbled from his mouth like forks falling from the kitchen counter. Even a short conversation could cause a woman to stare over his shoulder, a squint wrinkling her forehead. And now he couldn't even talk with Janet. The first two times Eric had been through chemo and radiation, he and Janet had been like a team, always pulling in the same direction, but now she misinterpreted every word he said, and a battle had developed over which one of them knew what was best for Eric.

When he returned with the cones, Mickey Mouse was standing in front of Janet, his hands on his cheeks. "Fuck off," she said.

Mickey threw his arms up in alarm and scurried away while Janet mumbled something about a fucking rat. "I wanted him to get away and have fun for a couple days," she said. "I didn't think he'd fall in love."

Carl thought falling in love would be better than sitting through Stitch's Great Escape, but he shrugged, handed her the cone. "It's her long legs," he said. He expected Janet to give him a disapproving look, but, if she heard him, she gave no sign.

By the time Eric showed up they'd finished their cones. He caught the looks, the way they studied his face, trying to spot any problems. "Sorry," he said. "We went for a walk." He nodded at his father, "You got sunburned."

During dinner Eric talked about the girl. Her name was Samantha. Sam, he called her. "She's staying at the Holiday Inn next to ours. I'm meeting her later by the pool. " He squinted at the Mickey Mouse clock on the wall.

"I thought her name was Laura," Carl said.

Janet looked at him as if he'd said something wrong.

Eric laughed.

Twenty minutes after Eric left to meet the girl, Carl said he was going out to stretch his legs, that the room was too cold. He patted his pocket to make sure he had the room key and then waited at the door when Janet signaled that she was coming, too. "Let's walk by the pool," she said.

On the other side of the palmettos that separated the Holiday Inn parking lot from the Best Western, they saw Eric and the girl. She was wearing a black bikini, waving her long arms, then poking Eric in the chest.

Carl stopped, but Janet moved a few steps closer to the fence that enclosed the pool. "Let's not bother them," Carl said.

Janet ignored him for a second, then turned around. "There's no lifeguard for Christsakes."

Traffic hummed on Memorial Highway on the other side of hotel. Carl took a step back. "Come on. They'll be okay."

Eric whispered in the girl's ear. She nodded and they both jumped in, keeping their heads low when they surfaced, so they could barely be seen. There was a splash as one of them kicked the water, and then her screams carried across the parking lot. Seconds later, the screams turned to laughter.

Janet stayed near the fence another minute before backing into the shadow of the camellia bushes.

Carl listened to the water lapping the edge of the pool and the girl's laughter. "I never talked with him about the birds and the bees," he said.

Janet gave a soft snort. "It's a bit late for that, don't you think?"

"I told him to keep his pants zipped. That's all. I said, 'Keep your pants zipped.'"

Back in their room Janet rubbed the goose bumps on her arms and fiddled with the dials on the air conditioner. "You can see his ribs," she said.

"I know."

Carl couldn't see them from the window, but he stood there looking out. "How old you think she is?"

Janet slapped the air conditioner. "Does it matter?" She went to the bed and flipped through the channels on the television, eventually stopping at a weather station. A line of thunderstorms was moving in from the Gulf, a nasty blob of radar green and orange growing larger. By ten, she was pacing the room. "He should be back by now," she said. "They'll be closing the pool."

Carl didn't blame Janet for being angry, but he was afraid to give into it himself. He thought getting angry would poison the time they had. "He's with a girl," Carl said. "He's sixteen."

Janet pulled the corner of the curtain back and pressed her cheek against the window, trying to see the Holiday Inn pool. "Would you mind?" she said.

Carl nodded. "Back in a minute."

"And if you see him, just make sure he's okay. He doesn't have to come back yet."

Carl waved that he understood and slipped out the door.

Large, white moths fluttered around the security lights as he stood in the shadows of the camellia bushes, close enough to the pool to hear the water gurgling down a drain. Eric and the girl were sitting next to each other, their feet dangling in the water. Carl figured there was no place else for them to go. As she talked her hands waved, pointed, and flapped in front of her. From time to time she leaned against him and pressed her head into the crook of his neck.

He envied them for the way they whispered back and forth and the casual way Eric draped his arm over her shoulder. He wanted to tell Eric that he and his mother were going to go out and wouldn't be back until midnight. He wanted to give them time alone, in private. He watched for another minute, then turned and walked back across the still warm pavement to the room.

He closed the door softly, said they were okay, that they were talking.

"You think he told her?"

"Don't know."

Janet sat on the bed looking as if she was trying to remember something. "He's never going to make love to a girl."

The statement surprised Carl although he'd been thinking the same thing. "I don't think so," he said.

After they flew home and he and Janet were in their own bed, he told her his idea. "I'm going to find a girl to sleep with Eric," he whispered.

Janet didn't answer, and Carl thought the idea had offended her, but he persisted. "It's not just the sex. It's…" he struggled to find the right word, decided there might not be any word for it, whatever it was.

He heard Janet breathing in the dark. "A college girl," she said. "No one cheap. She could come to the house while we're gone. Can you do that, can you find someone?"

Carl propped himself up on an elbow. He was surprised at how quickly the discussion had raced ahead of his own vague plans. "Maybe," he said. He was a small-town, southern Ohio cop and finding someone young and attractive and willing to drive to their place would be difficult, maybe impossible.

Janet was still thinking. "No one strung out on drugs. You have to be careful about that. No drugs. No diseases either. And Eric mustn't know. He can't know we arranged this."

Carl wasn't sure how they could do that. He wasn't sure if he could find the right girl. He tried to read Janet's face but couldn't see her in the dark. "I'll try," he said.

Although he knew he was breaking several laws and there would be hell to pay if his plan was discovered, it felt good to be doing something. He first asked for help from a friend in the county sheriff's department, who gave him several names and places and didn't ask any questions, but Carl had no luck. The women were either too old, too cold, too made-up, or too skimpily dressed. On the second day he talked with the desk clerk at the town's one motel, who, for twenty bucks, gave him a name and pointed him in another direction. An hour later he was sitting in the student union of Hocking College.

The girl approached cautiously, like she might be walking into a trap.

"I'm Carl," he said, trying to put her at ease.

She didn't take the seat next to him but remained standing, ready to run. "I'm Carol," she said. "Carol White."

But the name Tina Smith was printed on the cover of her notebook. Her brown eyes were clear and bright behind dark framed glasses, and she had a wide mouth with pretty lips. She looked like a teenager in her jeans and pink flip-flops, and Carl worried she might not even be eighteen.

"So, you're a student here?" he asked. The name on her notebook, Tina Smith, was familiar, but he couldn't place where he'd heard it.

"I'm studying art," she said, which didn't exactly answer his question.

"This is for my son," he said, running a hand over his forehead, which was beginning to peel.

The girl cocked an eyebrow.

"I was hoping, we were hoping, my wife and I, that he wouldn't know we . . ." He glanced out the window behind the sofa. A groundskeeper was blowing leaves into piles next to the sidewalk.

"Arranged this?"

"Yes, arranged."

She looked away and smiled at an old man, probably a professor, leaving the cafeteria.

"He's sixteen."

She turned to leave. "Sorry."

"Please," Carl said. "Sit for just a minute."

She hesitated, then sat next to him on the sofa.

He had planned on only saying that Eric wasn't well, but, once he started, he couldn't stop. Nearly ten minutes passed before Carl stopped, shrugged as if there was nothing more he could say.

She frowned, perhaps out of sympathy or perhaps trying to gauge whether his story was true.

Carl waited for a couple students to pass. "He's not allowed to drive and he's not happy about that, but otherwise he's handling it okay, I think. He's been to Disneyworld and my wife keeps renting movies for him to watch, mostly comedies. They're just distractions." He looked away, momentarily embarrassed. "He's a teenage boy."

"How long?" she asked.

"A couple hours, longer if possible. It's not just sex. I want him to have . . . " He tried to find the word. "A connection. Yeah, a connection."

"No, how much time did the doctors say?"

Carl nodded rapidly to indicate he understood. The question had come up numerous times before with friends and family, but he was never sure how to answer. He was afraid that saying *not long* or *before Christmas* might cause it to happen sooner than later. He felt as if any answer was betraying Eric. He gave the girl his stock reply. "We don't know."

The girl stared at an abstract painting on the opposite wall. Blue triangles and a red ball. She had long fingers and unpainted nails. No rings. No watch. "I'm a cop," he said. "This is a personal matter. I need your help."

"I thought you were a cop," she said. "I can spot them."

Carl wanted to ask how but was afraid of the conversation going off track and her taking off.

"Where would we meet?" She crossed her legs. A pink flip flop hung from her toes. Her feet were tan.

Her matter-of-fact manner caught Carl off guard. He'd expected her to play him along, act reluctant so she could ask for more money. She sat facing him, her knees only inches from his. "Our home," he said. "I've got a map. It has my office number on it. This Saturday? Would Saturday be okay? My wife and I'll be gone from ten until about five in the afternoon. I'll pay extra for you to drive to our place. It's a half hour from here. Forty minutes at most. You can pretend you're lost."

"Lost?"

"Lost. Come to the door and ask for directions. Get him talking."

She studied the painting again, then nodded to someone in the cafeteria. She pushed her glasses higher on her nose, an act that Carl thought might be a signal. "Okay," she said. "You have the cash?"

Carl nodded.

"Three hundred. Drop it in the bag by my foot. Don't be obvious. She looked at the map he handed her. "Saturday."

"His name is Eric and—"

"I don't need any more information," she said.

Janet thought he'd been tricked. "What makes you think she'll show up? How do you know you didn't hand money over to a girl we'll never see again?" She shook her head as if she couldn't believe he'd fallen for the arrangement.

"She'll be here," Carl said. "She'll show." He was going to add that she was an art student and had pretty teeth, that of all the women he'd seen, she had the prettiest teeth. Instead, he asked, "Where's Eric?"

Janet looked out the window above the kitchen sink. "Listening to music in the garage with Darrel and Tubby." She grimaced. "I'm not sure about the hooker. This may be a bad idea. Saturday?" Janet and her best friend, who lived on the west side of Columbus, were meeting, an outing that had been planned for weeks and was an attempt on her friend's part to give Janet a chance to "catch her breath."

Carl didn't like Janet calling the girl a hooker, and it bothered him how quickly she'd changed her mind. He wanted to mention that their being gone was the plan. They couldn't very well sit downstairs while Eric and the girl were up in his bedroom.

"Everything will be fine," Carl said. "I can be home in five minutes if he needs me."

Saturday morning, a few minutes after Janet pulled out of the drive, Eric woke up with a bad headache. Carl pulled the curtains, put a cold washcloth on his head and gave him a Darvocet, then went to the door and watched for the girl. But by ten Eric was up and other than feeling a little lightheaded said he was okay.

"You sure?" Carl asked. He looked pale and there were dark circles under his eyes.

Eric sat at the kitchen table with the morning paper. "Well, the headache's gone." He looked up from the sports page and sighed as if gathering himself for something important. "You know what the best thing was?" he asked.

Carl shook his head, thinking the question was about Disneyworld.

Eric waited so long before answering that Carl thought something had happened, that maybe he'd had a seizure.

"Dunking a basketball." He flipped his wrist, mimicking the motion of a dunk. "It was like flying. I think the best things are like flying. That's my insight."

Carl fought the urge to tell him he'd be dunking basketballs again. Eric had made them promise two things: no phony hopes and no photographs. "You got up there," he said.

Shortly after ten Carl left for the station. He worried that Eric's two buddies, Tubby and Darnell, might stop over. He worried about Janet, how she'd gone cold on the idea of the girl coming to the house and had considered staying home. He worried that the girl wouldn't find the house or that she wouldn't come at all. Most of all, he worried about Eric. He felt guilty, angry, scared, alone, helpless, and something else he couldn't identify. Time had been going crazy, speeding up and slowing down, stopping, then zooming forward so fast he felt as if he were on a merry-go-round that had spun completely out of control. He pushed the coffee cup to the corner of his desk. He sure as hell didn't need any more caffeine. He tapped the tip of a pencil on a yellow legal pad.

Tina Smith. He looked through the filing cabinet and found the name in a folder from several years ago. Tina Smith's father was in prison for killing a woman in Columbus during a botched robbery. Tina and her mother moved to the area shortly after the trial to escape the publicity.

Carl wondered what he'd done. Had Tina agreed because he was a cop and she thought he had some special power over her or her father? Or maybe she would use this to get something other than money from him.

The clock on the wall ticked.

A little before two his cell phone rang. He grabbed it thinking it was Eric.

"I'm home," Janet said. "I got here just in time. The girl was getting out of her car. I sent her away."

"What?" Carl said.

"It would have been a mistake. Eric never needs to know." She waited. "Carl? You there?"

"I'm here," he said.

Three weeks later, Eric died.

Throughout the fall and winter, Carl felt like he had the flu. He hurt all over, his knees, his elbows, his back, his neck. It took all the energy he had to go to work. Grief and guilt. It was impossible to tell where one left off and the other started.

By December, Carl and Janet were spending their nights staring at the television, unable to remember what they were watching, often going the entire evening without looking at one another. Once, after a particularly long quiet spell, Janet said, "It would have been wrong." Another time she said, "If you get terminal brain cancer and you want to fuck some girl, go ahead, but it would have been wrong for Eric."

Other arguments took place quietly, Janet thinking that having sex with a girl he'd only known for a few minutes was morally wrong, that they wouldn't have wanted Eric to fuck a hooker had he been well, and Carl thinking that it was different for boys, that the girl should have come to the house earlier.

In bed, Janet's foot never bumped his ankle. He stopped laying his hand on her hip. It was as if any physical intimacy might remind them of Eric and the girl, what could have happened and what didn't.

Sometimes, when the phone rang, he thought it was Eric calling, asking for a ride home from basketball practice or saying he was going to stop by Tubby's. Sometimes, in the mornings after he showered, Carl stopped at the door to Eric's room to tell him it was time to get up. Sometimes, Janet pulled three plates out of the cupboard. They were unable to talk about Eric at the same time. It was as if one person's grief might overwhelm the other's. When Carl reminisced about the time Eric hooked a seagull while fishing, Janet stared at the wall, tight-lipped, like she was holding her breath beneath water. Carl walked out of the room in the middle of Janet repeating Eric's often told story about Mr. Houser, his math teacher, setting fire to the wastebasket.

They went to a counselor. Carl didn't think it would help, but Janet insisted they go, so he did.

During one of the sessions Janet brought up the incident with the girl and how she'd sent her away. "I did the right thing," she said.

The counselor looked at Carl, expecting him to respond. When he didn't, Janet answered for him. "He thinks it would have been more than a fuck. He thinks it could have been—what do you call it, Carl?"

Carl struggled to find the right word, shook his head that he couldn't remember. Sometimes it felt as if she were accusing him of wanting to sleep with the girl.

The counselor said these things take time, that it's natural to second-guess decisions made when caring for a dying child.

"Like flying," Carl blurted out, pleased he'd found the word.

The counselor and Janet exchanged a puzzled look.

But Janet had been right. He thought the girl could have given Eric more than a fuck although it seemed to him that even a simple fuck would have been better than Disneyworld. He played Janet's version of the events that fall afternoon, the way she had come home just as the girl was arriving. Four hours. Eric had been home alone for four hours and for what? He and Eric could have gone for a walk or sat by the pond.

The following spring Janet began going out with her friends, meeting them for coffee and a bagel on Saturday morning. She planted red petunias along the side of the house and hung a hummingbird feeder near the back window. Occasionally, in the evenings before the mosquitoes came out, Carl shot baskets at the lopsided hoop on the garage, feeling in the brief time between the ball leaving his fingertips and clanging off the rim, that he was Eric.

The day after Mother's Day, a day they did their best to ignore, he told Janet he had business at the college and might be late. He arrived at the student union shortly before eleven. The odds were against him, but he'd been sitting on the sofa only twenty minutes when he saw her walking toward the cafeteria. She was wearing a pink T-shirt with "ARTS" in small, black letters across the breast. Her hair was cut short. She looked older than before, more academic. "Tina?" he said.

She cocked her head briefly, frowned, then pushed her sunglasses up on her forehead.

Carl thought she might be going by another name. "Tina?" he repeated.

She looked puzzled.

"My son. We talked last fall. My wife."

"Your son?" There was a flash of recognition. "I'm busy," she said, an edge to her voice, a warning that he should leave her alone. She turned her shoulders as if squeezing by someone in a crowded room although at that moment they were the only two in the lobby.

"He died," he said.

She stopped.

"Eric, my son. Last October."

Three girls came out of the cafeteria laughing. She pulled her notebook close to her chest, waited until they passed, then shook her head as if anticipating his next question. "I need to be going. I'm very sorry about your son."

Carl felt like he was on a stage and had forgotten his lines. He held up a hand for her to wait. "My wife should never have sent you away," he said. "It was a mistake."

"Please," she said. "Not here. Not now."

Carl dropped his voice to a whisper. "He was alone. I should have stayed home or asked you to come earlier."

She nodded at the sofa near the steps. They went there and sat facing each other although not as close as during their first meeting. A tray clattered to the floor in the cafeteria. "She was angry," she said. "Your wife. I thought you said it was her idea, too."

"She changed her mind."

"I have a class. I don't understand what you want."

Carl looked at the back of his hands as if he might find the answer there. "I don't know."

A tall boy with a wimpy goatee walked by, glanced at the girl. A mower roared beneath the window. She waited.

"He was dying and alone, and I spent the day staring at my desk." Carl wanted to tell her about Eric, how he'd teased the girl in Florida or that he had been able to mimic anyone's walk, or that he collected pictures of clouds, all stupid things. He shrugged. "I'm sorry. This was a bad idea." He shifted his weight forward, ready to stand and walk away.

"I was there," she said, letting the backpack slip off her shoulder and onto the floor with a thud.

"What?"

"I was there. Before eleven."

A bubble of hope rose inside him and then broke. He'd heard his share of alibis and stories that ran contrary to the evidence. "My wife sent you home," he said.

The girl cocked one eyebrow.

"She sent you home," Carl repeated. "She sent you home before you ever got in the house."

The girl took a moment to begin her story. "I went back for my lipstick. It fell out of my purse. I was careless."

Carl stared at her, waiting for her to look away or give him a tight grin, something the speeders and drunks always did. "You're making this up," he said.

She glanced out the window, as if she were remembering or maybe searching for ways to develop her story.

"You told him you were lost?"

"Lost? No."

"I told you to tell him you were lost, I said—"

"I had a better plan. You should include some truth when you're lying. My father taught me that."

"What did you tell him?"

She pressed her lips together, raised her eyebrows, a clear signal that she wasn't telling or, Carl thought, perhaps there was nothing to tell.

"He had on"—she closed her eyes—"a pair of jeans. A white T-shirt, I think." She touched her breast, the spot over her heart, with an open hand, a gesture that liars seldom used.

Carl looked at her as Eric might have. Intelligent eyes, wide mouth, large white teeth. A girl comfortable in her body. Yes, she could have been convincing.

She bit her bottom lip as if she were debating whether to go on.

"Please," Carl said.

"There were birds outside the window."

"Birds?"

"Crows. They were squawking, I mean really squawking, and he thought it was funny. We couldn't stop laughing. A nervous thing I think."

Carl tried to remember if there had been crows around the house last fall. Maybe. They sometimes came swooping out of the cornfield behind the pond. "Crows," he said. He imagined a cool breeze coming through the bedroom window, the warm skin of the girl. But then he remembered the way liars always go on too long, adding details to their story after they should have stopped.

The girl rubbed a thin, white scar on her earlobe between her thumb and forefinger. "I was there," she said.

On the other side of the window, students walked to class, and pink blossoms fell from the cherry trees that lined the walk. In a moment he'd stand, give her a little nod, say thanks, walk to his car, and drive home in time for lunch. He rehearsed the movements in his head, so he could get them right and not make a fool of himself. She'd walk down the hall, out into the sunshine, and he'd never see her again. He'd never tell Janet that he'd talked with her. He'd say he'd given a lot of thought to her sending the girl away, and she'd done the right thing. He, too, could be convincing and a lie can be such a comfort.

OTHER WORLDS

Mysteries of the Universe

The premonition hits as I walk down Park Street to the university. One foot up in the air and bamm! Knocks me back like a punch in the gut or a mysterious pain in the chest. A premo that sends a chill down my spine despite the warm spring morning. I try to shake it off. I have things to do.

Crows squawk in the maples and oaks, a holy racket. In the distance the university band rehearses for the halftime show of the first home football game four months away, another holy racket. The smell of fresh baked bread and donuts drifts from Sweet Melissa's Bakery on Lake Avenue.

I try to wash the ugly inkling, the déjà before the vu, out of my mind by concentrating on the cottonwood fluff floating in the air, the noisy crows scolding me, the fat dandelion blossoms blanketing the lawn. A large limb from a sycamore tree has fallen across the sidewalk in front of the physics lab. The dew-covered grass in the shade of the red bricks and ivy of Rodman Hall needs mowed. Cleaning up downed limbs, mowing, trimming, mulching flowerbeds, seeding the muddy areas around the greenhouse. Maintenance stuff. My job. Need to get everything looking tiptop for graduation.

The premonition gnaws at the sunny day. It's a dark thundercloud threat just over the horizon, lightning flashing, thunder booming. I hope it's a false warning, a fake forecast.

I've had a few, both good and bad, fake and not. Take the one when Sloane and I were camping in the Boundary Waters, our first date, although we didn't think of it as a date. We'd known each other three weeks. Morning fog blanketed the campsite so thick we couldn't see the water a few feet beyond our beached canoe. Dew dripped from the needles of the pine trees, landed on the rocks with little plops. I closed up the camp stove, and we took our cups of coffee inside the tent, sat on our sleeping bags with Yogi hunkered down bear-like between us. "A moose," I mumbled a few minutes later, just as the coffee was beginning to cool.

"What?" Sloane asked.

"Outside the tent," I said. I hadn't heard a thing, no hooves crunching on pinecones or sloshing through water, no chomping of aspen, no snorting. Pure premonition.

Sloane gave me her Ph.D. in theoretical physics look. I couldn't even recite the title of her doctoral thesis, which had something to do, she explained, with cosmic rays called Oh-My-God particles. I had no clue what Oh-My-God particles were despite her attempts to explain, but I took comfort in her admitting no one else knew much about them either. Sloane says space-time is curved by gravity and that virtual particles pop in and out of existence, but she doesn't buy into premonitions, prophesies, omens, or signs.

Holding onto my cup, I crawled to the tent flap and flipped it aside. Ten feet away and staring at our red canoe was a giant moose although, I guess, all adult moose are giants. I touched my finger to my lips and pointed. Yogi, curious but cautious, watched, sniffed the air. No growl or bark. The moose grazed around our campsite then stepped into the lake and urinated, which sounded like a bucket of water being dumped or a waterfall dropping from a respectable height. "Premonition," I said a bit smugly.

Sloane shook her head.

I tried throwing a little of her theoretical physics stuff at her. "Didn't you tell me yesterday as we were paddling across the inlet that quantum things in the future can influence the present? Maybe the future moose in front of our tent signaled it would be there."

Sloane smirked. "Future events influencing the present is only true in the quantum world," she said.

Sloane is driven in an indoors/office/journal reading sort of way. Although she had traveled to conferences in several countries and a dozen major cities, this was her first camping trip. I wanted to ask how one thing could be true in her quantum world and not ours, but the moose had moved on, and she was packing up, preparing to move out.

Later that day, the moose day, two young women wearing nothing but hats paddled by us, which at first I thought had nothing to do with this story.

"Morning," I said, doing my best not to focus on their as yet un-tanned breasts.

"Morning," they answered.

And then one called out. "Russ?"

I squinted, trying to bring the woman into focus. "Cass?"

She waved and I waved back. "Cass," I said again.

After they'd rounded a bend behind us, Sloane, sitting in the bow, turned, cocked her eyebrow. "Well? Someone you know?" She spoke softly as sounds carry over water, and she didn't want the topless paddlers to hear.

I was still processing seeing Cass here of all places. Saying yes, I knew her, would invite more questions.

"I'd worry about mosquitoes and sunburn," I said, "but it's a free world."

Sloane puzzled over my answer for a second. "In the spirit of sisterhood," she said, and then facing forward, pulled off her sweatshirt and bra.

I stared at her back, the way it narrowed near her waist, the smooth skin, the soft bumps of her spine. "Oh, look," I said, pointing at an island behind us, tricking her into turning around. "Thought I saw a bear."

She squinted at the island, and then at me. "Yeah, right," she said, daring me to stare.

A bare-breasted theoretical physicist sitting in the bow of my canoe. Who could have imagined?

Sloane says we met by mistake, but I say we have a cosmic connection.

When the science department has a lecture I attend. I like seeing slides of galaxies, nebulas, the colorful clouds of Jupiter. When I was in high school we had careers day, and I signed up for cosmetology, which I had mistakenly assumed was cosmology. The instructor, a woman with fluorescent blond hair and bright red lipstick, asked each of us to describe our interest in cosmetology. "Wrong class," I muttered.

Sloane, applying for a position in the physics department, gave a lecture on dark energy and mistook me for another prof. Instead of wearing my maintenance clothes, boots and a blue shirt with Russ, my name, stitched in red above the pocket, I wore a sport coat and tie, having come from my niece's recital. (Lucy's only ten and plays the violin.) After the lecture I complimented her, and she asked about my research focus. "Oh, I go in circles," I said, referring to mowing the lawn, but she thought I was talking code for work with the Hadron Collider. We went to dinner where her mistake became obvious as I had no clue what she was talking about: Hilbert space, vacuum energy, the fine-tuning problem. She laughed when she discovered I mowed the lawn, and when we returned from our Boundary Waters canoe trip, she moved in with me, saying I was a mystery and she liked mysteries. We've been together nine months, something my mother calls a pregnant amount of time.

Her look: white blouses and not a wrinkle in them. Black skirts that show off her long legs. She's thin and has reddish-blond hair, which she wears in a no-nonsense, professional above-the-collar cut, a style the instructor in the cosmetology class might have liked. Her lips stretch across perfect teeth and her hazel eyes sparkle when she smiles. She doesn't wear glasses, which is surprising her being a theoretical physicist who is always buried in a book.

Anyway, all this has little, maybe nothing, to do with my premonition, but, as Sloane says when describing her quantum particles, we really have no idea what is real and what isn't, so I've included it here in an effort to be as honest as possible even though honesty is a seldom admired characteristic today despite lip service by politicians, religious folk, the FBI, and the Boy Scouts.

The spring semester is almost over, and dandelions cover the campus commons. Oscar Kurt, the head of maintenance and my friend, ordered ten gallons of Roundup and asked me to spray last spring and fall. I don't trust Roundup despite assertions by DuPont that it's safe. I got rid of it, burned it in the incinerator, then sprayed the lawn with water. I don't understand Oscar's love of Roundup. He was in Vietnam, got sprayed with Agent Orange, which has been linked to his Non-Hodgkins Lymphoma and was made by Dow Chemical, which is now part of DuPont, so you'd think he'd be suspicious of chemical sprays and chemical company claims.

Oscar catches me as I approach the maintenance shed. Before he went through chemo, he looked like Samuel L. Jackson what with his big smile, bald head, and the gap between his front teeth. But he's lost weight, and now has sunken cheeks and a scrawny neck. I think he's going to warn me about the dandelions, which isn't really a premonition as much as a hunch. There's a difference.

Oscar owns a hangdog expression and gets right to the point. "Sloane," he says. "How do you feel about her getting the trip?"

Trip? I squint. "What trip?"

He waves his hand in the air, trying to remember the name. "The Antarctica thing."

I don't know about any Antarctica thing. Sloane going to the South Pole is something I can't imagine. Our canoe trip to the Boundary Waters was her equivalent of going to the moon.

"Maybe I shouldn't have said anything. Maybe she's going to surprise you."

"When?" I ask.

"Maybe over dinner. I don't know."

This is the way Oscar talks, expecting you to fill in between the lines. He also has spells, gets confused, maybe the chemo, maybe something else. He calls me Wes sometimes when I'm Russ, maybe a beginning dementia thing, maybe exposure to Roundup. "No," I say, "I mean when is the South Pole thing?"

He looks up in the trees, maybe trying to remember, maybe watching a squirrel. With Oscar, everything is maybe. "This summer, I think. Going to be there six months." He pauses, points at the dandelions and shakes his head. "That Roundup ain't doing shit," he says. And then remembering, "Maybe she said something and you forgot."

Sloane works late, sleeps late. Much of her work is done at her office desk. Most of it is math without numbers, just letters and squiggly lines, sometimes a graph. I've seen it. Why would she want to do that in Antarctica? "Must be a mistake," I say. "She's a theoretical physicist. They go to conferences in big cities, sit indoors. They don't go to the South Pole. We're going camping this summer."

"Can't be in two places at once," he says.

But you can, or at least those quantum things Sloane talks about can. Here and there at the same time. Unbelievable. It's like a habit with them.

I haven't talked with Sloane since lunch yesterday. She nudged me with an elbow to the ribs when the alarm went off this morning, but she went back to sleep before I rolled out of bed, so we haven't had time to talk about the South Pole or her being in two places at once.

Oscar, like me, has not had much luck in his love life, and he tends to be cynical about relationships. That's why he worries about Sloane. He thinks she's stringing me along, which has nothing to do with the string theory of the universe she often mentions.

I dismiss Oscar's off-hand warning the way I dismissed ten gallons of Roundup and this morning's premonition. I toss Antarctica in my mental incinerator. Melted. Gone.

I'll stop by Sloane's office later, after I take care of the sycamore limb blocking the sidewalk next to the physics building, after I pretend to kill the dandelions. We'll have lunch together, and she can tell me something new, maybe explain how gravity curves space or how those quantum things can be in two places at once. I'll ask about the Antarctica thing, which goes to show my mental incinerator is not working.

When Sloane goes for a walk to ponder, she takes Yogi. What a sight! Yogi weighs 140, twenty pounds more than Sloane. When we went to the Boundary Waters, Yogi and I swam despite the water being so cold my fingers, toes, and personal body parts went numb. He stayed by my side, kept an eye on me. That's the Newfoundland way. His chin is white and his eyes are milky. He is slow to get up, and he sits gingerly, but he loves to swim.

Students greet me as they head to their classes. "Hi, Russ, "Morning, Russ," they say. My name is stitched in red letters above the pocket of my blue shirt, which I have already mentioned, so they know me and that I can unlock their dorm room doors when they forget their keys. They watch, a few do, as I cut up the sycamore limb and haul it away. Sycamores love water and the physics building is on high dry ground, so I have no idea what the tree is doing here. I sometimes wonder what I'm doing here, too.

Anyway, by the time I finish taking care of the limb and pretend to Roundup the dandelions, it's lunchtime, and I enter Rodman Hall, the physics building. Sloane's office is on the third floor, the floor with the view of the football stadium and the river. I knock on her door and it swings open. "Oh," she says. "Is it that time?"

In the beginning we ate lunch together a couple times a week at one of the tables in the faculty lounge off the cafeteria, days when she didn't have meetings or a class, but we stopped doing that for reasons I don't know. It happened. A mystery. When the weather warmed up and everything began to green, we sometimes walked home and had lunch there, sat on the back steps and watched Yogi sniff around the yard, cock his arthritic hip on the bushes.

Today, however, the day of the bad premonition, I order delivery from Busy Day Café before heading to Sloane's office. I don't have to specify what we want. It's always the same. "Lunch for Russ and Sloane," I say. I'm in Sloane's office five minutes when Jerry whose-last name-I-don't-know shows up with the white bag holding our sandwiches, a vegetarian wrap for Sloane, a steak sandwich for me. Sloane drinks Coke despite my warnings about it being a lot like Roundup. I drink water.

We make small talk. She's amused by my granting amnesty to the dandelions but otherwise she's preoccupied. Sloane is desperate to understand the universe. "Is it those Oh-My-God particles?" I ask, nodding at the papers on her desk.

She goes, "What? No. Just thinking. We need to talk." She looks at the office door the same way Oscar went blank staring off at the squirrels and for a second I think something is going around, a distraction bug or virus.

I wait for the talk we need to have but none comes. I avoid the Antarctica thing because I don't believe it's true and because I'm afraid if I ask it will be, sort of like those quantum things that come into existence when you observe them. There's a connection here I can't explain. "Hey," I say, trying to drum up a little enthusiasm. "I'm looking forward to the lecture tonight."

She sips the Coke, leaving a smudge of lipstick on the straw. "Oh, Russ, are you sure you want to go?"

I take a bite of my steak sandwich. It's huge. Her veggie wrap is green and small. Maybe that's how Sloane stays so thin. I'm confused as to why she thinks I might not want to go. I go to all the physics lectures. I like hearing about the unknown, and I've not made a fool of myself by asking a question, stupid or otherwise. I just listen. "Sure," I say. "I'm going."

"Going where?" a voice behind me asks.

Rocky, the grad student she's supervising. I want to say, *Oh my god, it's Rocky*, but what I actually say is, "Hey, Rock. The lecture tonight."

Rocky's eyes never look straight at you but off to the side, like you're really six inches to your left. He's thin and pale and cultivating the Einstein look with his wild hair. He wears dark-rimmed glasses and needs to change his name or switch his major to geology.

"Excuse me," he says to Sloane, stepping behind me and my steak sandwich. "Do you have time this afternoon to look at my calculations . . ." and then his voice trails off as he mumbles things like Planck's constant, dimensions, and vacuum energy.

Sloane gives me a look that says she needs to take care of this and it would be a good time for me to run home and let Yogi out for a few minutes. She can say all that with one look, a twitch of an eyebrow, pursed lips.

I grab my sandwich and thermos of water—no plastic bottles for me— and nod to Rocky, who flinches despite my not touching him. I save the last two bites of the steak sandwich for Yogi, who will give me a look that says thanks.

Later, after sitting on the back deck with Yogi and him giving me the look that says thanks, I walk back to the university where right off I'm confronted by two students, a young man wearing flip-flops and a tie-dyed shirt and a tiny, wide-eyed, granola-type girl, who may or may not be his girlfriend. Both are holding cell phones, like this might be the way they talk to each other. "Russ," she says. The tone of her voice suggests she's locked herself out of her room. Again, this is not a premonition but a hunch based on voice, body language, and her blocking my path.

"What can I do for you?" I ask, and she points at the grass, at the tiny pink flags warning that the dandelions have been sprayed with an herbicide and they should stay off the lawn for twenty-four hours.

"You're poisoning the environment," she says. Her tie-dyed friend nods.

"It's not poison," I whisper. "I put flags there so everyone would think I sprayed the dandelions." I hope this doesn't get back to Oscar who would be sorely disappointed in me.

The girl, wearing a Greenpeace badge on her jean blouse and half a dozen silver rings dangling from her ears, takes a defiant stance. "Herbicides are poisonous," she says. She snaps a picture of the pink flags with her cell phone. "You're killing microorganisms in the soil. Animals will track this back to their homes. Birds will eat poisoned worms."

I bend down and snap off a dandelion. She jumps back like I'm going to attack her with it. I bite the dandelion. She gasps. The guy stares at me. "Cool," he says.

For a second I think the dandelion has a sickening sweet smell, a bitter taste. I worry that Oscar came out with more Roundup, real Roundup and not water, and dowsed the dandelions. I pick another, a fat, bright yellow one with moisture still clinging to the bloom. I sniff. There's no sweet smell and the blossom tastes like salad without the dressing.

The girl is confused. Maybe I'll die in front of her and maybe I'm telling the truth. She tugs at the sleeve of her boyfriend's tie-dyed shirt, and they slip away, careful to not step on the grass.

Another thing I learned from Sloane was that things, quantum things, exist only when they interact with other things. If they don't interact, they don't exist. I asked Sloane to explain. She started, took a deep breath, stopped. "Electrons, photons, all the tiny bundles of energy that make up atoms, don't exist unless they interact with something."

"Yeah," I said. "But how is that possible?"

"It's hard to explain," she said.

Although she assured me I had nothing to worry about, I welcome these interactions with students. We exist!

A lot of the things I learned from Sloane came during our canoe trip to the Boundary Waters. "What came before the Big Bang?" I asked as we paddled across a smooth stretch of water. Yogi's ears perked up like he wanted to hear the answer too.

"There was no before," she said. And then she asked, "What's wrong with those trees?"

"They're aspen. Probably the Aspen Blotch Miner. It's an insect."

"Will it kill them?"

"Probably not. And how can there be no before?"

"There was no time."

We paddled close to shore. The wind had shifted and we were alert for any sudden change in the weather while I tried to grasp how there could be no time. A few seconds later—see, there's time—I touched my finger to my lips and pointed at the bird swimming ahead of us.

"What is it?" she whispered.

"A loon."

We went back and forth all afternoon, me asking questions about the universe, how an electron could be in two different places at the same time, what is dark matter, and Sloane asking questions about the Boundary Waters, what were the smooth rocks where we beached the canoe, why was the area so rich in iron ore, what was the story of the Native Americans who had lived here, and where had they gone.

I've heard dozens of science lectures, and I've read a few books, but I'd never had a chance to ask questions of an expert. My job during those science lectures is to be quiet. Talking with Sloane I felt the way a music lover taking a canoe trip with Adele or Prince might feel, like a football fan talking with Jimmy Brown, the greatest running back of all time.

We fell into something special on that trip, if not love, something moving in that direction. Sloane had a wicked sense of humor and several times we laughed so hard we almost tipped the canoe. At night, after the mosquitoes quieted down, we'd stretch out on the smooth slab of rock along the shore, hold hands and stare at the stars while Yogi snored beside me. I tried to imagine a universe that went forever and then tried to imagine one that didn't. Was there intelligent life somewhere out there staring back at us? How did this universe get started and why were we here? Sloane was looking for the answers. Loons called back and forth, their songs both beautiful and haunting.

Sloane talked all winter about the two of us going on a return trip to the Boundary Waters. "I want to see a bear," she'd say. I have the permit and a couple weeks off in August. That's why I don't think Antarctica is a real thing.

I get ready to mow despite the mower's roar annoying the professors who are trying to teach electricity and magnetism, particles and waves. A few professors have become so outraged by the mower's roar that they fight back. We have battles. The physics professors have threatened to shoot me with lasers and turn on powerful magnets that would suck the fillings out of my teeth. I let the tractor backfire and make an extra sweep past their windows when these things happen. I hate cutting the dandelions, but a job is a job, so I make sure the mower deck is secure, fire up the tractor, and begin making loops around the green. Mowing is a good time to think.

Do premonitions have an expiration date? How can you tell the fake from the real? These are things Rozzi and I argued about when we were on patrol outside Kandahar. Rozzi claimed if you never told anyone your premonition it wouldn't come true. He hoped it might keep at bay the nightmare scenarios we all foresaw. He also said premonitions had no expiration date. I argued everything died sooner or later, even premonitions.

I can't shake this morning's premonition, which is like a bad dream, a disturbing movie playing on a screen behind my eyes. Made me feel hollow. If this premonition were a movie there'd be sad music playing, maybe a cello or bagpipes, maybe the theme from the movie Starman at the moment Jeff Bridges is about to leave and never come back. I would describe it except for hoping Rozzi was right. If I keep it under wraps it won't happen.

I go around and around, the circle of mowed grass growing smaller with each loop. I take comfort in knowing the dandelions will be back. The sun is fat and bright, the first really hot day this spring, and my neck is burning.

After work I walk home, I call Sloane's office as I put a pizza in the oven. "Russ," she says. "Sorry. I'm going to dinner with Dr. Franz and Dr. Ahman before their presentation tonight. We're on our way now."

I hear other voices and laughter in the background. "Okay," I say. "I love you."

"Okay," she says. "Got to go."

I eat half the pizza. Yogi's bones are tired, and he ignores my offerings of the crust.

As I walk toward the lecture hall the whistling of the spring peepers and the smell of fresh cut grass cheer me although they do not wipe out the ghost of this morning's premonition. When I arrive the room is half full of grad students and their friends. I don't spot Rocky's wild hair. The two giving the lecture and the physics faculty have not yet shown up, still hobnobbing, I suppose, at the Other World Tavern across town.

I take a seat near the front and save the seat next to me for Sloane although she will probably sit in the first row with the other physics professors. This does not bother me. I understand how she might want to lean over and whisper a quantum question or comment to one of her peers who will whisper theoretical things to her.

Five minutes before seven they show up and take their seats in the first row. Sloane turns in her seat, spots me and nods. I wink back and let out my breath, which I didn't realize I'd been holding. After long introductions the lecture begins.

The first speaker, a physicist responsible for experiments with photons, explains that when two quantum particles are close to each other they become entangled. They can then be sent their separate ways and still, somehow, maintain a mysterious connection when thousands, even millions, of miles apart.
I like the idea two particles can remain connected when far apart. I think Yogi and I have that. I hope Sloane and I do, too.

Next up, is an older woman who repeatedly swings her head to the side to get her long, going-to-gray hair out of her eyes. Her theory is that the universe is a hologram, nothing more than a projection stored in a two-dimensional membrane surrounding the universe. "Which is real?" she asks. "The three dimensions we think we know or are we and our world like the images in a mirror, mere projections?"

I can't sit still any longer. Maybe it's the weight of the bad premonition. The thought that we are nothing more that images is too much. I raise my hand.

The woman smiles, leans forward and nods.

"But we're more than images," I say, hoping I haven't missed the entire point, hoping, too, I'm not embarrassing Sloane. I tap my chest, the spot over my heart. "I'm solid."

The woman nods a few more times to acknowledge my question. "But you aren't solid. You are mostly empty space. And that very tiny bit of you made up of protons and neutrons and electrons? Well, they're not solid either. They're bundles of energy that pop in and out of existence. It's a great mystery, isn't it?" And then there are more questions, eager grad students wanting to impress their professors and each other. I stop listening. When the lecture is over, when the speakers have been thanked and everyone heads for the door, there's a tap on my elbow.

"Russ?" she says. "You okay?" She sits, one vacant chair between us.

"Are we entangled?" I ask.

"That happens only in the quantum world," she says.

"Are you going to the South Pole?"

She doesn't appear surprised by my question. "Yes. I don't like the cold and it's outside my realm of experience. But I'm looking forward to it." She glances at her group as they wait for her by the door. "We can talk later."

I say I understand although I don't. I want to ask about our trip to the Boundary Waters and if she plans on living with me when she comes back from the South Pole, but I already know the answers. Sloane pats me on my knee and says she has to run.

The auditorium is mostly empty when I leave. On my way out the door I bump my elbow. Solid.

As I walk across campus my mind races from one thought to another. Yogi is having trouble getting up and down and this may be his last trip to the Boundary Waters. A couple sitting by the lake laugh and lean into each other. The spring peepers sing. Usually I take comfort in seeing the night sky full of stars, but tonight is an exception. I feel alone. Temporary. My premonition haunts me. I feel like I'm no more than a character in someone's story, and I might, my entire world might, at any moment, blink out of existence.

Area 52

Rocky and Sloane are in the backseat. Oscar's riding shotgun. I'm driving Sloane's car, a state-of-the-art hybrid SUV with more gizmos, buttons, and doodads on the dash than the cockpit of a stealth bomber. I have no idea what most of them do, and I'm afraid to touch a knob or dial for fear I'll get ejected through the roof or send a distress signal to the local fire department. "You drive," she said, handing me the keys when it was finally decided we were all going to join Larry, my brother, in welcoming my father home. She doesn't want her car sitting idle while she's in Antarctica studying cosmic rays, and she's trying to sell it to me, her housemate, man friend, her whatever.

"We need a little more air back here," she says.

I look at the switches, dials, buttons, and knobs. Oscar leans forward, his hand poised momentarily in front of the panel and touches an icon.

"Thanks," Sloane says. "That's better."

But it's not. Sloane's in the back seat with Rocky. What is she thinking? She told Oscar to sit up front because of his long legs. I don't like the arrangement. Everyone going to greet my father is a terrible idea. Sloane took the call and said my brother asked her to come, told her to bring a friend. "The more the merrier," he said.

So here we are, cruising down Route 7 along the Ohio River. I don't feel merrier, and I don't understand why Rocky was included or why he agreed to come. He doesn't know my father. He doesn't know why my father was in prison unless Sloane told him, which she swore she'd never share. Maybe I'll tell Rocky my father murdered a man who flirted with my mother. I'll tell him jealousy and violence run in my family.

I'm taking the long way to my brother's. The drive along the Ohio River is more scenic. That's my excuse, the reason I have given everyone in the car. It makes me sound like a good guy, which I'm not. The real reason is that this way takes a half hour longer than the more direct route, and I want to postpone our arrival as long as possible.

"What do you think, Rocky?" I ask, nodding toward the river. I'm trying to hide my anger that Rocky came along.

"About what?"

I glance in the rearview mirror. Rocky is looking at Sloane, not the river. At least I think he's looking at Sloane. Rocky's eyes don't point like they should. "The river," I say. "The Ohio River."

"Ah yes, very pretty."

Sloane and Oscar have met my mother and brother, so they know what they're getting into. Rocky has not. None of them have met my father, whom I've seen only during brief visits to the prison where we sat at cafeteria tables, where he sometimes sobbed, not over killing the woman but how he missed driving his old Pontiac.

I thought Sloane and Rocky might talk science, cosmic rays, dark matter, maybe the false vacuum problem, all mysteries of the universe. But no. They swap university gossip. Who did this, who said that, what about the new dean, and was the secretary fired or did she quit? Oh, and the budget cuts. How many faculty positions will be eliminated?

"How about dark matter?" I say to the backseat. Dark matter, what it is and finding it, is Rocky's thing.

"What about it?" Sloane asks.

I don't know what about it. That's why I asked. Invisible stuff that makes up most of the matter in the universe and no one knows what it is. How is that possible?

Rocky comes to the rescue. "We have a number of experiments going that may give us some answers." He and Sloane mumble back and forth.

"A few physicists don't think it exists, but Rocky will find it," Sloane says.

Oscar gives me a sly smile. He's dressed in bellbottom jeans and a blue button-up shirt two sizes too big for him although the baggy sleeves and blousy nature enhance his bald, old hippie, gaunt look.

My brother lives in a secluded area near the Hocking Hills surrounded by trees and large rock outcroppings. This being a Sunday he will have spent the morning preaching and praying. Despite there not being a cloud in the sky my sister-in-law and mother will have been fretting over the possibility of rain and if they should set the table inside or outside at the picnic tables.

I try to prepare everyone for the visit. I explain that when my brother prays before a meal the food is cold by the time he finishes. Rocky, the Muslim, laughs. Oscar, the Buddhist, laughs. Sloane, the lapsed Catholic shushes me, says I should be kind. I don't practice any religion, which may be why I'm unkind, thinking things like Rocky should take a swim across the river. I warn them: "My family is strange."

"We're all a little strange," Oscar says. He starts humming a song by The Doors.

A barge pushes coal up the river.

I lived in the Hocking Hills during my last year of high school, and I loved the ledges and the steep, wooded hills. Deer and wildflowers, mushrooms in the spring. Old Man's Cave, Rock House, Conkle's Hollow, Ash Cave. Only the whisper of the wind in the trees and the crunch of leaves beneath my feet. My brother was never happy there. He never walked into the forest or climbed one of the rocky slopes. But there he is, living at the edge of the park in a house that looks like a Yellowstone lodge. The gate at the end of his drive is open, and gravel crunches beneath the tires as we pass through the shadows of red pine.

I take a deep breath, park between my brother's big-as-a-bus camper and the First Church of Hope and Salvation van.

Oscar takes it all in, the house, the three-car garage, the massive stone chimney, the manicured lawn, the piles of food on the picnic table, the flowers along the front of the house. "You say he's a preacher?" he whispers.

"Evangelist," I say. "Has his own television and radio show."

"Think it's too late for me to become an Evangelist?

"You're a Buddhist," I say.

Oscar rubs his chin. "Maybe I could be both."

My brother steps out the front door followed by Ruth, my sister-in-law, and my mother. "Freak!" he says. "Let's go. We're late."
Been here thirty seconds and I'm already puzzled. "Late for what?" I look at the food on the table. I'm hungry.

"Pick up Dad," he says, jangling keys in his hand. He points at the church van. "All aboard!"

"I thought we were meeting him here."

"No, no. We're picking him up at the gate. Come on. We're running late."

Larry holds the door of the van open, and I make introductions as one by one we climb in.

The fifteen-passenger van has barely enough room for Sloane, Rocky, Oscar, my brother, Ruth, their four kids, my brother's two friends—him with slicked-back hair, shiny, soap-scrubbed face and her of too much perfume—and me. "We can wait here," I offer. It's a selfish offer. I don't want to ride in the van with Larry driving. The high center of gravity makes these vans dangerous, and my brother drives like he's aiming the Olympic luge down the chute, leaning this way and that while hoping to make the next curve. Besides, someone should guard the food on the table.

"No, no. Dad wants to see everyone at the gate," he says as he swings behind the wheel.

Helium-filled balloons float against the roof of the van. I want to point out that there's only so much helium on the Earth, rather in it, and no more can be made. Once it's released in a cheap balloon it's gone forever. Liquid helium super cools super magnets in MRI machines. It's needed for scientific research. Before I can speak up, my brother slams the door shut and we're off. Sloane's in a seat wedged between my mother and Rocky. Oscar and I sit behind them. If I was wearing a tie, I could loop it over Rocky's neck and strangle him.

We are in a church van on the way to pick up my recently paroled father from prison while my brother tries to lead us in a campfire church song I don't know, but he and my mother insist I do. The song, he says, is how we'll greet my father.

If I were my father I'd ask to stay in prison.

The singing quickly peters out, and Larry gives us a running monologue about the area, which I only catch bits and pieces of, while he takes curves and hills too fast. The van leans hard to the left, then hard to the right. I want to warn him about the van's high center of gravity making it easy to flip over.

He says, "We're running a little late."

My father has been in prison for eighteen years. Ten more minutes will not matter.

The curves come fast and hard. I feel claustrophobic, too warm. The collar of my t-shirt presses against my throat. My stomach goes down when we go up a hill and up when we go down. I try to focus out the front windshield, but the view is obscured by balloons and heads. We go too fast over a hill and for a few seconds my stomach floats behind. I know where the prison is, and I know how to get there, but Larry is taking a different route. I can't tell where we are or how far we have to go. I need air.

"Freak?" Oscar whispers.

"Later," I say.

He leans closer. "You okay?"

I can't look at him. I can't turn my head. I have to concentrate.

"You don't look so good," he says, this coming from a man who recently went through radiation and chemo.

I try to focus straight ahead. "Open the window," I say.

Oscar wrestles with the window latch without success. "Won't open," he says.

The van is too warm. I can sense Sloane and Rocky turning in their seats, looking at me. Larry takes another curve too fast, another hill where my stomach does a flip. Breakfast is churning high in my chest. I burp and taste last night's hotdogs.

My head feels like it's been detached from my body. My stomach gurgles in protest. "Stop!" I yell.

Larry doesn't stop.

Sloane leans forward in her seat. "Stop the van! Russ is sick."

Larry whips the van to the side of the road and slams on the brakes, throwing us forward in our seats. I open the door and fall out before we come to a full stop. I land on the ground, stumble, and step away from the van.

"We can't wait," Larry says.

"I'll stay with him," Oscar says.

"It's your driving" Ruth says. "You're taking these hills like a maniac."

"He always got sick in the car," my mother says.

"Just trying to get there when Dad's released," Larry answers. "We wouldn't be late if Russ had gotten here on time."

Sloane passes a water bottle to Rocky who leans out the door and hands it to Oscar. "Hey," my brother calls out. "We'll pick you up on our way back."

The door to the van slams shut and they're off.

"You okay?" Oscar asks.

I'm embarrassed. "The breeze feels good," I say. Thirty-two years old and I get motion sickness like a three-year old. I hate this sign of weakness in front of Rocky. What the hell was my brother thinking, driving like a fool over these hills?

"I wasn't feeling so good either," Oscar says.

I look around, try to get my bearings. I'm not familiar with the road. We're surrounded by a forest, and there's a large boulder with a flat top perfectly situated in the shade. When we sit on it the coolness seeps through my jeans.

"Getting your color back," Oscar says.

"Thanks for keeping me company. I'm feeling better although I'm not ready to get back in the van."

Oscar holds out the bottle of water. "Drink?"

We pass the bottle back and forth. A breeze rustles the leaves. Crows, high in the tree across the road, scold us. "And you?" I ask. "How are you? I mean how are you really?"

He doesn't answer right away. It's like he's taking inventory of how he is. "I feel pretty good today. I'm not going through chemo again. Once was enough." He shrugs as if that's all there is to the story.

We're quiet for a few minutes, thinking and waiting for the van to return with my father.

"From a gung-ho marine to a peace-loving hippie to an old bald guy," he says. "It happened fast."

"You're still a peace-loving hippie," I say.

He nods. "You've got that right. And a marine."

As if a gunnery sergeant gave us the command to stand, we both get to our feet and walk down the hill. I'm not wearing a watch, so I don't know how long the freedom van has been gone, but it should be coming back this way soon. "Sorry for dragging you into this," I say.

"No, no," Oscar says. "It's been entertaining."

We stop at an old forest road that cuts into the hill and disappears in an overgrowth of trees and lush fern. It looks inviting. "Better not," I say to myself as tempting as it is to follow the road and see where it goes

A cop car comes down the hill, shoots past us. The brake lights come on as it goes around the curve. A few seconds later the car appears again, going much slower. Even before the lights begin flashing, I get a bad feeling.

"What'd you do now?" Oscar asks.

My first fear is Larry's flipped the van, and someone told the cops Oscar and I were out here waiting. My second thought, upon seeing the casual way the cop climbs out of the cruiser, is that we're about to be harassed.

"Fellas," the cop says.

The voice is familiar. I can't identify it, but I get a sinking feeling we're in trouble.

He's wearing dark shades that hide most of his face and walking with an exaggerated stride, maybe from the weight of the gun, handcuffs, radio, pepper spray, flashlight, taser, baton, and bullet proof vest. He's chewing gum the way a cow chews its cud, his jaw making big circles. One hand rests on his belt, ready to draw. He could have stepped straight out of *Smokey and the Bandits*.

"Russ?" he says.

I hesitate, not sure I want to admit I'm me. "Yes?"

He steps closer. "I'll be damned. It's you. Don't recognize me, do you?"

"Your voice," I say. "Your voice is familiar but . . ."

He takes off the sunglasses. I see his face but it's his name tag that seals the deal. Charlie Palm. Last time I saw Charlie was when he punched me in the jaw at a high school party. "Charlie!" I say, trying to sound as friendly as possible. He has a gun.

"Russ!" He opens his arm and gives me a man hug. "Wow," he says, stepping back but still gripping my shoulders.

I'm at a loss for words, so I point to Oscar. "My friend, Oscar," I say. "And this is Charlie Palm." I don't know what else to say. *An old high school friend?* Not even close. *A bully who made my life miserable?* True, but not wise. He has a gun.

"I was the high school troublemaker, got into all kinds of trouble," Charlie says, finishing my thoughts. "Russ was the science guy."

Oscar shakes Charlie's hand and since the gun has not been drawn and the cuffs are still on his belt I began to relax. A little.

Charlie spits out his gum, a wad the size of Denmark. "Can't believe it's you. I gotta tell you, this is weird."

"It is," I say.

"No, I mean seeing you here, next to the trailhead. This place is like Area 51, you know, the place where the UFOs landed out west. This place might be even more special. I call it Area 52. It gives me goosebumps." He holds out his tattooed arm to show me the goosebumps, but I don't see any.

He changes the topic, asks what we're doing on the road, no car. He asks how I've been, if I'm married. He holds up his hand, shows us a wedding band. "Eight years," he says. "Have two boys."

We go back and forth with small talk, how we're waiting for my brother to pick us up and how long Charlie's been with the force, and then he returns to the goosebumps and how he can't believe he saw me here, at this trailhead of all places. He tilts his head in the direction of the old logging road. "Only person I've told about what happened up here is Amy, and I'm not sure she believes me. But you were into science and I trust you."

Sloane would question the idea that I'm a man of science. Oscar and I work maintenance at the university. Why Charlie would trust me is a puzzle.

"Back there," he says, pointing up the trail, "'bout a mile in. I was camping. My twenty-first birthday. I was planning something could have gotten me in a heap of trouble. I won't say what, but it was big. I was up late, poking the campfire, working out the fine details of this thing I was going to do when the rocks around the fire began to glow. I shit you not. I'd had a bit to drink and thought the heat from the fire was responsible. I touched a few stones, and they were cool." He stops, looks at Oscar. "You won't breathe a word of this, right?"

Oscar makes the motion of zipping his lips.

"Yeah, okay. Well, more rocks began glowing, marking a path deeper into the woods. You know, like in the Handle and Grabel fairy tale with the breadcrumbs. Maybe I was curious or in a trance. I followed the trail. I came to a small clearing, and a beam of blinding blue light shot down out of nowhere. I couldn't move. I swear, one minute I'm standing in the woods and the next I'm sitting in a special chair with a doohickey thing clamped on my head."

Charlie stops again, studies our faces to see if we believe him. Oscar and I respond with sincere looks, eyes wide open, a little slack-jawed, as if we're about to say, *Wow*!

Satisfied, Charlie continues.

"It was them." He pauses to point at the sky. "They never hurt me, but there was a funny odor in the air, sort of like electrical wiring burning, you know? I woke up back at my camp, in the tent, in my sleeping bag twenty-four hours later. Afterward, I had no desire to do this deed I'd been planning. I went a hundred and sixty degrees the other way. And here I am."

I don't know what to say. He has a gun.

The cruiser radio squawks. A female dispatcher requesting something for a 10-16.

"Sorry," Charlie says, as he spins around and runs to the cruiser. "See you."

Seconds later, the siren is on and he's racing up the hill.

Oscar and I exchange a look. "Glowing rocks." Oscar says.

"Doohickey thing clamped on his head," I answer.

"Handle and Grabel," Oscar says.

Oscar and I wait. I don't know what's taking Larry so long. Maybe they've changed their mind about releasing my father. I'm annoyed with my brother and embarrassed to keep Oscar out here waiting like this. What was Larry thinking, driving these roads like a maniac? And Sloane! She's off with Rocky to greet my father as he gets out of prison while I stand beside a road in the middle of Area 52.

Oscar and I walk up the hill to the spot where we were dropped off. Walking feels good. The cool boulder where we were sitting is in the sun and warm to the touch. We're about to climb the embankment and wait in the shade when the van appears, slows as it approaches and then stops.

The door opens. Everyone is laughing and talking, enjoying ice cream cones. The helium balloons are gone. My father sits next to my mother. I haven't seen him since Christmas, and I'm reminded again of how he's aged in the eighteen years he was locked up. He's all bones and angles. His chin, brow ridge and hooked nose give him a hard edge. If he was a Rorschach test, your answer would be knife. "Hey, Dad," I call out.

"Russ," he says.

"Sorry for keeping you waiting," Larry says. "There was a long line at Dairy Queen."

Sloane leans over the seat, holds up her nearly gone vanilla cone. "I would've got you one," she says, "but I was afraid it would melt by the time we got back to you. Here, want the rest of mine?"

I shake my head although a chocolate cone would taste good.

"You'll never believe who I just saw," I say.

Everyone starts laughing, even the kids, and I don't know what's so funny. It was like I told the funniest joke they'd ever heard. I was directing the comment to my mother who had turned in her seat to face Oscar and me.

"I told you," Larry says. "I told you."

Everyone laughs with renewed enthusiasm. Sloane chokes on the last bite of her cone and covers her mouth to hide a smile.

Oscar swings the door shut and we start down the road.

"What?" I ask. "What's so funny."

"You," Larry says. "I told them about your imaginary girlfriend. Is that who you saw?"

"What?" I ask, but before he explains I know what this is about. Larry never met Cass the summer she lived with her grandparents across the street. He was away at camp. Then, when I ran into her again years later, he was off at seminary school. Every time I mentioned her, he accused me of having an imaginary girlfriend and said she was a figment of my imagination and desires. Maybe he was jealous. I'm not happy, him bringing this up.

"What was her name again?" Larry asks. "Carol? Cathy? Started with C or K."

"She wasn't, isn't, imaginary," I say.

"Cass!" he says. "Her name was Cass." He laughs so hard he momentarily loses control of the van, and the tires hook the edge of the road, throwing us to the side before he quickly corrects and throws us the opposite way.

"Keep driving like that," I say, "and I'm going to throw up in your van!"

"Larry?" Ruth says, a soft warning.

"Cass," he repeats. "Does he still talk about his imaginary girlfriend, Sloane?"

The question is like asking if you still beat your wife. No matter how she answers it looks bad.

"No," she says. "No imaginary girlfriends." She grins like she's doing me a favor.

"It was embarrassing," Larry says. "This continued all the way into high school and college."

I want to remind my brother about what happened between Cain and Abel, and if he keeps this shit up history will repeat itself.

"Mom," I say. "You met her, the girl across the street when I was in seventh grade? Dad?" I've resorted to asking my parents to stick up for me in this stupid argument with my brother. Pathetic.

"Sorry, honey," she says.

My father's tracing a line on the window and doesn't answer.

I can't let this go, not yet. "I saw her at the ballgame in Cleveland the other night. She was sitting behind the bullpen."

My brother laughs so hard I worry he'll lose control of the van. "I don't believe it," he says. "I don't believe it." Ruth shushes him but he ignores her.

I wait a few seconds and then change the subject. "I was going to tell you we saw Charlie Palm."

"Charlie Palm," Larry says. "We saw his cruiser fly by. Fine man. Found God. Goes to our church. He's one of our deacons."

I want to say he found aliens, too. I don't.

Larry prays as we sit around two over-sized picnic tables loaded with food, which, including the potato salad, has been sitting in the sun for over two hours. "Bless this meal," he says. I figure I'll believe in the power of his prayer if no one gets food poisoning. He continues to pray and after a few minutes my mind wanders and my eyes open. Rocky's on the other side of the table across from Sloane, and I catch him wink at her. They both quickly bow their heads and pretend it never happened. My brother continues to pray, thanking the Lord for each person present. "Thank you, Lord, for bringing my father home, so we can be together again. Thank you, Lord, for my mother, who . . ."

A tom turkey emerges from the trees and slowly walks toward the drive, its beard almost touching the ground. A breeze ruffles the paper plates. I want a slice of the cake, which I saw on the kitchen table when I went inside to use the bathroom. Chocolate. Three layers at least.

"Thank you, Lord, for Freak, my brother, and please take away the sickness that plagued him earlier as we . . ."

The tom struts as he stares at his reflection in the hubcap of Larry's Lexus. He holds his wings in a display of dominance, turns sideways, and comes back to the hubcap again and again, strutting, threatening the tom he thinks he sees, torn between the real and the imagined.

I do a lot of thinking as Larry prays. After I have a slice of that chocolate cake, I want to return to Area 52, hike up the trail, build a campfire and wait for the rocks leading off into the woods to glow. I'll follow that glimmering path as far as it takes me, and, when the brilliant light comes out of the sky and aliens whisk me up into their ship, I'll beg them to take me home, wherever it is I came from. I'll bet Cass will be there.

HIGHER MATH

Anticipation

What I recall most often about the first year of art school is not Cody's giant coffee mug exploding in the kiln or Luanne accidently gluing the seat of her pants to her studio stool. What I remember best is the old guy, who looked like Samuel L. Jackson, sitting on the sidewalk next to me, a teenage white girl, as I laughed uncontrollably.

He looked at me as if I'd lost my mind.

"What's so funny?" he asked as I rocked back and forth, flirting with the fine line between laughing and sobbing.

I tried to answer but couldn't speak. I took a deep breath and kicked the sheet of plywood resting at our feet. "Lifting heavy things makes me laugh."

"What?"

I waited until another wave of laughter passed. "It's like when a doctor taps on your knee, and you kick. It's a reflex. You should have heard me when I tried carrying a mattress into the dorm."

Folks driving down Palm Avenue in their spotless SUVs and convertibles slowed, stared, and then, perhaps convinced I'd gone mad, quickly drove on, which threw me into another fit of laughing. The more I tried to stop, the harder I laughed. Then he began to laugh. His body shook. We laughed so hard we cried as we slumped against the brick front of the thrift store.

Despite the California sunshine and it being my birthday, I'd had the blues for weeks. Y2K threatened that the world would collapse in a month, and Slick made what I thought would be my favorite class, studio painting, a living hell. Slick. Not Professor Slick. Not Tom, Dick, or Harry Slick. In a premature attempt to coin a name to suit his anticipated fame, he'd gone to a one-word, single syllable name. Like Cher, Sting, and Seal, there was now Slick.

During every class he stalked the studio, hands in the pockets of his paint-splattered apron, his pretentious ponytail hanging like a limp dick. With his sun-bleached hair and dark tan, he looked more like a kook surfer than an art professor, and though he'd often been spotted at Malibu and Huntington Beach, a board tucked beneath his arm, no one had ever seen him riding a wave. In the studio, he prowled from one student to the next like a cat ready to pounce as he spouted *Slickisms: Sweet and pretty has no energy. A painting of your fond memories becomes a sentimental Tom Kincaid or Frederick Morgan. Abstract art is not a goddamned photograph. Paint the dark side.*

We heard these countless times, and then as he circled the studio, he came out with a new one: "*Art is competition. A mountain gets smaller the closer you get to the summit. Only a few can stand at the top, and you don't get to the top if you're roped to the past.*"

I turned to Cody and whispered, "What the hell is he talking about?"

Cody, whose easel was next to mine and whose family lived in Richmond, Virginia, two hours from my parents' place in Norfolk, told the class during first day introductions that he was often mistaken for Tom Cruise. This comparison may have gone to his head as he frequently quoted lines from Cruise's movies—*I feel the need . . .the need for speed. You complete me.* And perhaps his favorite: *Show me the money* in which he often substituted anything at hand for money: *painting, beer,* and once, *leg.* He also mimicked Cruise's exuberant mannerisms. Despite his Cruise-ness, when he asked if I saw the resemblance, I lied and said no.

"Les jeux sont faits," he said.

In French Lit—if you want to be an art major, you need to learn French or Italian, better yet, both—we read Sartre's *Les Jeux Sont Faits,* which made the point that what's done is done. Going back to the past doomed the main characters, Eve and Pierre, to a loveless death. My mother, sister, roommate, and brother had been telling me a version of the same thing. *Forget Russ—you only knew him a couple weeks, my mother warned. You'll never see him again,* my sister, the junior at the University of Virginia, declared as I was about to drive across country to art school. *Get a real boyfriend,* my roommate said. *You can't steal second with your foot on first, Jeremy,* my younger brother, liked to repeat. *Move on,* they all said.

Our family had been "moving on" from the time I was a toddler. From MacDill Air Force Base to Nells to Clark to Wright Pat to Malmstrom to Langley. We were masters of moving on, and I'd tried to anchor myself—*grounded* might be the more appropriate Air Force word—to a woodsy area in southern Ohio where, while spending a few weeks with my grandparents one summer, I met Russ. After arriving in California, I decided to take everyone's advice—including Sartre's—and try to move on, to become a California girl, whatever that was.

As much as I thought I was moving on, my paintings reflected the past: my grandparents' front porch, the apple tree in their backyard, and a bike leaning against a tree along the Ohio Canal—I liked the juxtaposition of the bike and the canal. Slick hated all my paintings, called them sentimental and pretentious. "Paint sex or violence!" he said. And then he laughed. "Or violent sex!"

Slick painted geometric abstracts in bold blacks and grays with an occasional slash of orange. He'd had exhibits in New York, San Francisco, and Santa Fe. Heady stuff, especially for someone who had only recently cracked thirty. He'd spent the semester guiding us through various approaches to contemporary art, and the pressure was on to have a successful final project.

I liked abstract art—Kandinsky, Pollock, De Kooning, and Kline were my favorites—but I didn't like Slick's. I hadn't told him, hadn't told anyone, but I had the feeling he knew. Rather than abstract paintings that pulled you in, his were a slap in the face, a poke in the eye, a chicken bone stuck at the back of the throat. I would have dared any of my classmates to stare at one of his paintings for a minute and not grimace. Couldn't be done. The only place I could imagine his artwork hanging was on a cell wall at Pelican Bay.

Based on my previous paintings, Slick said I'd lived a charmed life, had never done anything dangerous, never done something I regretted, or suffered a serious loss, and it was reflected in what he called my "failed attempts to do something profound."

Charmed life? Maybe. Never done anything dangerous? Hmmm, not so fast. Never suffered a serious loss? I won't go there. Never done something I regretted? How about telling Cody, after I'd had too many beers, that one of my high school paintings came true, that it had predicted the future. It wasn't a great painting by any stretch, not even good, just a couple sitting on a rock while watching a comet streak overhead. Four months later I was the girl in the painting, sitting on a hilltop boulder with Russ, a guy I hadn't seen in years, watching the comet Hale-Bopp streak overhead. Cody wouldn't let it go, had taken to calling me Sibyl and fortune-teller, and pressuring me to paint something sexy to see if it, the sex, would happen. Then, in front of the class he told Slick about my painting that saw the future.

Slick smirked. "You should do well on the final assignment, Cass. The theme for the school exhibit is anticipation."

Weeks later, as he slowly circled the room, I stared at the sheet of 300 lb. cold press on my easel. I had five practice paintings and a dozen sketches in my drawer, hoping Slick would finally have a kind word about my work. For the final assignment I'd painted a combination of Van Gogh's Starry Night and Klimt's The Kiss, featuring a young couple inches apart about to embrace—where else?— beneath a starry sky. I painted the couple in red because I didn't have gold on my palette.

Cody and I became allies the first week of class after Slick called us the East Coast contingent and made snide comments at what he called our East Coast sensibilities, but our alliance was weakening under Cody's repeated jokes about my future-telling muse. His constant airing in public what I'd told him in private was destroying the mystery and magic of that painting. I never told him about the second painting that had also caught a glimpse of the future, the one of a teenage boy walking down a railroad track at night. I learned my lesson minutes after telling him about the first.

As Slick slowly circled the room, we turned over our notecards, revealing for the first time the title of our paintings. Cody lifted his chin at my notecard: The Next Kiss. "Really?" he asked, bouncing his eyebrows.

It wasn't the next kiss with anyone specific. It was the next kiss that counted, that really counted. How could I explain that? I shrugged.
Cody held up his arm and pointed at a long scar that ran from his wrist to his elbow. "Totaled my first car," he said, flashing his dazzling and expensive smile. (He'd had his teeth capped to resemble those of Tom Cruise.) He started to pull

up the bottom of his shirt to reveal another scar but decided against it when Slick looked our way. The title of his painting was The Next Crash. Now that I knew its inspiration I could, with a lot of imagination, make out a shattered windshield, tires at odd angles, and a boxy, misshapen car resting on its roof. All black and gray except for orange and yellow flames licking what may have been the engine. Slick, I thought, would love it.

Listening to Cody, I lost track of Slick's progress around the studio until I felt his presence behind me the way some must feel the Grim Reaper's scythe sweeping through the air before their last gasp. During his lap around the studio, he only stopped if your work was brilliant, or an utter failure—or if you had large breasts. I wasn't brilliant, and I didn't have large breasts.

"The next kiss?" Slick asked.

Without looking, I sensed the rest of the class pause, look up from their work and wait for my answer.

"Yes."

"That's all the poor boy gets, a kiss?"

Slick must have had redeeming qualities. Maybe he was good to his mother, and there were a few in our class who claimed to like him.

"If you think a kiss can't be special," I said, "I feel bad for those you've kissed."

He smiled, and I worried he might have taken my comment the wrong way, as an invitation of sorts.

Okay," he said and then clapped his hands for everyone's attention. "Time for critiques. We'll start with Cody."

This meant my painting would be the last to be reviewed although Slick had already set it up for negative comments with his smug remarks. We were expected to react to each painting after it was put on display at the front of the room. Cody's got mostly positive comments although a few thought the choice of medium—pastels—was not appropriate for a painting with such violence. No one wanted to trash someone's work, knowing the negative comments might come back tenfold on their own. Slick thought the painting had energy. Cody nodded and returned to his station next to me.

"You anticipate what?" Slick asked when it was Annie's turn. She blushed. He rested a hand on her shoulder and smiled. "First Time," he said, announcing her title. There was laughter, but the comments quickly became supportive, Jennifer and Leanne making it clear that the abstract painting with colorful fireworks and a lightning bolt cutting the black background captured their feelings the "first time" and the painting "spoke" to anticipation.

Whatever.

Lydia with the long black hair and scooped-neck top was next. Slick smiled, rested both hands on her shoulders as he nodded at her painting. When she announced the title, The Second Time, he clapped his hands and said there'd obviously been collusion between her and Annie. Slick and Lydia locked onto each other's eyes. Creepy. Her anticipation was expressed with red strings forming a Fibonacci curve. Was that a psychedelic spiderweb? A fishing net? And those large dots with tails, were they spiders? Captured insects? Sperm? I didn't ask. Most comments were favorable.

When Jake went to the front of the studio and put his painting on the easel, he said, "The title of my painting is "The Eighty-Third Time," which got a lot of laughs, mostly from the guys. Federico's painting was Y2K and suggested doom. Mbo's painting—my favorite—was titled Earthquake and showed buildings shaking and falling. We were, after all, in California.

I began to relax. My classmates were being kind with their comments.

When my turn came, I carried my painting to the easel at the front of the room. "The Next Kiss," I said. I started to add that the painting was a take-off on Klimt's The Kiss and Van Gogh's Starry Nights, but before I could explain Slick waved me off and motioned for the class to make comments. Cody said the painting had raw emotion. Dixie thought the two bodies about to embrace beneath the starry sky worked well. Someone else complimented the choice of colors, especially the dark blue background.

Then it was Slick's turn. "What's the focus of the painting?"

Silence.

"Look!"

The fluorescent lights hummed. A siren wailed in the distance.

"There is no focus! The kiss? The starry sky? The colors clash. The painting is corny, and it's not even a kiss."

He took the painting, held it up for everyone in the class to see, dropped it on the floor, and walked on it. There was a gasp. He twisted his foot as if he were stomping out a burning cigarette, his shoes leaving dirt and scuff marks. My face felt like it was on fire. I was angry. Embarrassed.

All eyes were on us. Weeks of work smashed. A big wrinkle on the foreground, a crease down the side, a tear over the couple and one corner missing. "Here," he said, taking my hand as if he were about to lead me onto the dance floor, signaling I should walk on it, too.

I couldn't do it and stepped to the side. I'd thrown out hundreds of drawings and sketches over the years, so I was familiar with getting rid of paintings and drawings that didn't work. However, I would have kept this one. It wasn't a Kandinsky or Pollock. I had no illusions about that. It wasn't the best painting in the class, but I would have hung it in my dorm room.

He pulled me to the side and my foot landed on the painting.

"There you go," he said, still gripping my hand. "For your next painting, explore a dark desire, nothing happy or sappy."

Was he talking about the painting or something else? Lydia glared as Slick held my hand.

"Throw it away," he said, pushing the paper toward me with the toe of his sandal. "Start a new one this weekend. Be ready to show us dark anticipation Monday." He winked.

Like a zombie, I stooped down, picked up the torn and stepped-on pieces, carried them to the large trash bin, while Slick clapped as if this was performance art and not studio painting. "End of class," he said.

I gathered my things and, without looking back when he called my name, left the studio. I'd been plagued by the blues for weeks, and Slick wanted me to paint the dark side? A self-portrait would have been perfect.

Cody walked outside with me. "That sucked," he said.

When I didn't respond he pressed on, nudging me in the shoulder, and reciting his movie lines. "The Next Kiss! Show me the kiss!"

"Please, Cody," I said.

"Your painting predicts it," he said. "Make it happen, the kiss, the mystery."

"The mystery is what I'm going to paint for Monday! I have two days to come up with something! I've got to get back to the studio tonight." It was almost the end of the semester, and I was tired.

Cody held up his hands like a cop stopping traffic. "Can I ask you a question?"

A pigeon flew up in front of us, barely missing Cody's head.

"You just did." I sounded more sarcastic than I intended. "Sorry. Sure, ask away."

"The guy in your painting?"

"Hurry," I said, seeing a break in the traffic. We raced across the street.

"Listen, I have to pick up a few things. How about we meet back at the studio later."

"Yeah, yeah," he said. "See you there."

I walked three blocks not having any destination or idea of what I might do next. I just wanted time alone. What upset me most wasn't Slick's criticism of my painting, but his throwing it on the floor and stepping on it. Next painting, whatever it was, would be on something he couldn't tear, a concrete block, a sheet of metal, maybe the studio wall. I was wrestling with different possibilities as I approached the site where a music store was being renovated. I passed the store—it was in what was considered the seedy part of town—almost daily on my way to run in the park. I'd never paid much attention to the contents of the dumpster blocking the sidewalk or the man in the fatigue jacket, who was always sitting nearby, tossing a baseball back and forth between his hands. A sheet of plywood protruded from the top of the dumpster.

The plywood was dirty, and bent nails stuck out of the corners, but it was a full four-by-eight-foot sheet, three quarters inch thick. Slick wouldn't be able to shred that unless he brought a chainsaw to class.

The disheveled man watched as I examined the plywood. "This yours?" I asked.

He looked at the dumpster and then at me.

"I mean the plywood, do you want it?" I thought he might use it to build a shelter, a lean-to.

He gave a disinterested shake of his head. Was he amused, annoyed, or plotting to rob me?

I tugged on the plywood, but it was wedged between boards, window casings, and pipes, and it didn't move.

The man, his legs crossed at the ankles, a cigarette hanging from the side of his mouth, watched through half closed eyes. "Need help?" he asked. His voice was deep and rumbled like it came from one of the tectonic plates shifting beneath our feet.

I needed help but was afraid of what he might do or want in return. He wore an old Marine fatigue jacket despite it being a warm afternoon. His hair sprang from his head like a mushroom cloud, and he might have passed for an old hippie if not for the dog tags hanging from a silver chain around his neck. He continued passing the baseball from one hand to the other. A nervous habit or potential weapon?

He appeared to be about my father's age, fifty, and judging from the dog tags and Marine jacket, may have been a Vietnam vet. He looked familiar, and by the way he squinted at me I thought he had the same feeling, that we'd met before, not just in my passing down the street.

I pulled on the plywood again and tried to wiggle it free. It didn't budge. I briefly considered finding Cody and asking him for help, but the plywood might've been gone by then. "Sure you don't mind?" I asked.

He rubbed his eyes as if having second thoughts on his offer to help.

"If we get it out, I can drag it back to school." I immediately regretted telling him I was a student, a girl far from home. It was late afternoon, the sky was overcast, and there wasn't another person on the street.

He stood and tucked the baseball in the pocket of his jacket. "I try to do a good deed once every century and time for this one is running out," he said, the cigarette clenched between his teeth. He came to the dumpster, eyed me before reaching in, and then swung the plywood out and onto the pavement.

He smelled of cigarette smoke and clove gum.

"I can get it from here," I said, stepping back.

He gave a slow nod that suggested he didn't think I could. He was tall and his jacket hung loose on him.

I tried lifting the plywood, but it was difficult to get a grip, and I only dragged it a few inches. "The art institute. It's four blocks. You sure?"

"I know where it is," he said.

I grabbed the front end, and he took the back, but we'd only carried it across the street when I dropped my end and began to laugh. The harder I tried to stop laughing, the harder I laughed. My knees went weak. I sat on the sidewalk and still I couldn't stop.

He looked at me as if I'd lost my mind. "You're one crazy girl," he said. Then he began to laugh. We laughed so hard we shook as we slumped against the brick front of the thrift store.

"I haven't," I said, weak and out of breath, "laughed like this in a long time."

He nodded. "Been a long time for me, too."

A police car slowed as it went by, and I waited for it to stop, for a cop to get out and ask what we were doing.

"Act normal," he said, smiling for the first time since I'd seen him.

Act normal? That sent me into another fit of laughing.

The car passed, and I took a deep breath. "I'm Cass," I said, hoping I wasn't being foolish giving him my name but thinking, if we had a connection, he might not give up on helping me.

"Cass?" he said, scrunching his face as if he were deciding whether I was telling the truth or that he might recognize me from a previous encounter. "I'm Oscar."

"Okay, Oscar," I said, "let's do it."

"Heave ho," he said.

My laughing stopped us twice more before we got to campus, but Oscar stuck with me. The smell of French fries and bacon came from the cafeteria as we passed, and I felt guilty, wondering if he was hungry and if he was living on booze and drugs. I kept waiting for him to ask for money and hoped the art building would be full of students and faculty members, but it was a late Friday afternoon, and no one was around. With a great deal of juggling and effort we carried the plywood up the steps. The studio smelled of oil paint and possibilities. He gave the sheet of plywood a skeptical look as we propped it against the wall. "What you going to paint?"

I looked at the plywood, hoping an idea would appear. "I don't know. The theme is anticipation. The professor told me to paint something dark, something violent or frightening. 'Listen to the dark side,' he said. I just want something he can't step on or rip up."

"He does that?"

I nodded. "Did it to mine."

"Paint something happy," he said.

"He doesn't like happy."

"Who doesn't like happy?"

"Slick. Professor Slick."

"Don't paint for him. Paint for yourself."

I attached a note to the plywood. *Do not move!* "I need a good grade."

"So, you paint for a grade?" He'd taken the baseball out of his pocket and was passing it back and forth between his hands.

"Let me treat you to dinner," I said.

"I'm good," he said, turning to leave.

"Wait! I don't want to eat alone. It's my birthday."

He stopped. "Guess that'd be okay."

I couldn't take him to the school cafeteria. Too many obstacles and stares. "Pizza?" I asked.

"Pizza's good."

We walked two blocks to Salvatori's Pizza on Palm Street. Oscar was quiet, sat on the other side of the table, and again I felt I knew him from a previous encounter. "So," I asked, "where you from?"

"All over," he said.

"Me too!" I answered.

We began comparing places. Ohio was one state we had in common.

"Tell me something about Ohio that made you happy. Maybe I'll paint it." I was just trying to get him to talk, say something that might trigger why he looked so familiar.

"Len Barker," he said.

"Who?"

"Cleveland pitcher threw a perfect game. This was in '81. I was there with my wife. Only thing could have made it better would've been a full stadium. Should have had a full house for that."

"But you were there."

"I was."

I started to mention that I'd never been to a baseball game, not a major league one, anyway. "You played baseball?" I asked.

A lopsided smile, a tiny gap between his front teeth. "Once upon a time."

He didn't eat like a starving man. His hands were clean and from time to time he paused between bites, cocked his head, and smiled.

I felt my gloomy mood, the melancholy and depression lifting. Oscar and I talked for an hour after we'd finished the pizza. School, baseball, Ohio, how we both loved to see the trees change in the fall. I told him about Russ and my painting that had predicted an evening we spent together watching a comet. "What are the odds?" I asked.

"That math is beyond me," he said. "Maybe you tapped into something special."

The entire time I was trying to remember when I'd previously met him. "I think we've bumped into each other before," I said, "but I can't remember where."

He shook his head. "This is the first time. We look familiar to each other because we'll meet again."

Before I could ask him to explain, he wished me luck with the painting and thanked me for the pizza. He grinned. "Today's my birthday, too." And then he left.

When I returned to the studio, Cody was there, eyeing the dirty sheet of plywood with my note attached.

"What?" he asked.

"If I tell you, it'll sound silly, and I may lose my motivation to do this."

I cleaned the plywood and then applied a thick coat of white gesso. I couldn't start painting until the gesso dried, so I went back to Cody's apartment and looked up Cleveland stadium online. It turned out that a new stadium had been built, and I liked the images of it. I was making progress.

The next morning, I painted a light blue background. The undercoat was dry by ten, and I began work in earnest.

I worked all day, taking breaks to let the acrylic paint dry and to consider what I wanted to do next. By Sunday I was putting in the people, colorful dots that filled the stadium. Late that night I'd almost finished, but something was missing. A stadium full of people. Where was the story? The anticipation? Cody asked if the painting predicted something and if so what. He said I should put a pitcher on the mound, a batter swinging. I thought about Oscar and his suggestion I should paint something that made me feel good, something happy. Viewing the painting was like seeing the stadium from center field. What if high in the stadium there was someone, say Oscar, not watching the game but watching me on this side of the painting? The idea excited me although I wasn't sure how to paint it. The faces were too small, just dots. But what if we, anyone looking at the painting, was looking through a pair of binoculars at that person. Yes! I immediately went to work. I titled the painting: *When I See Oscar Again.*

I'd invited Oscar to the exhibition and was watching for him when Cody stopped to say he was dropping out the next semester. "You're what?" I asked.
Cody struck a Tom Cruise pose. "I'm joining the church of Scientology," he said. "It'll help my art."

Before I could ask questions, Slick showed up. Oddly, I felt sorry for him, and I wasn't sure why.

He stared at my painting, paused, and shook his head. "Where's the anticipation?" he asked.

"Well," I said.
He leaned forward and as he waited, I walked away, hoping to find Oscar. I looked for him without success, and two days later, a couple classmates helped me carry the unsold painting down to the music store, where I propped it against the dumpster.

The Problem with Numbers

Speeding up Interstate 71 with Oscar. Goodbye rolling hills of southern Ohio. Hello flat fields north of Columbus, land pancaked by a monster glacier back in the time of mastodons and woolly mammoths. I look over the cornfields, try to imagine that wall of ice. It gives me a chill. "Can you feel it?" I ask.

Oscar looks out the window. "Feel what?"

"The cold air coming off that long-ago ice sheet."

"I feel it," he says. "Thought it was the air conditioner blowing on my legs."

Closer to Cleveland we pass strip malls, outlet malls, fast food joints, and tall, mirror-sided office buildings. Billboards line the highway and exit ramps shoot off in all directions. Condos and gas stations. Asphalt and steel.

A song has been running through my head all day, an overture to a premonition. This happens.

Cleveland and the Yankees, Oscar and I have tickets because Rocky couldn't go. Too busy. Sloane couldn't go either. She teaches in the university's physics department with Rocky. It's hard to be annoyed with Rocky after he gave me tickets. Still, I try.

Sloane, who has lived with me seven months and will soon leave for Antarctica to study cosmic rays, laughs at my unscientific thoughts, my premonitions, any suggestion of magic. "Everything can be boiled down to numbers," she says.

Oscar and I work maintenance at the university. Oscar is old, seventy-three. I'm thirty-seven and in my prime.

Sloane and Rocky are members of the Association of University Scientists. Some members bought season tickets for Cleveland home games. We'll be sitting with them, these scientists, and I'll eavesdrop on their conversations. "Maybe they'll discuss the Fine-Tuning Problem," I say to Oscar.

"Fine tuning what?" he asks.

I try to explain it the way Sloane explained it to me. "If any of the constants in the universe, those numbers that describe all the physical laws and forces, were the tiniest bit different,"—I hold up my hand, thumb and forefinger pinched to emphasize a teensy-weensy amount—"life couldn't exist. How is it our universe has all the right numbers?"

"Doesn't sound like a problem to me," he says.

Oscar practices Buddhism. He accepts the temporary nature of things. He goes with the flow and dresses like the hippie he once was. He's chewing clove gum and the spicy smell fills the cab.

As I turn into a parking lot four blocks from the stadium, I pat my shirt pocket, making sure I've got the tickets. "Don't forget your binoculars," Oscar says, nodding at the console between our seats. "They look dandy."

I'm about to explain that they were a gift from a girl I once knew, but the story gets complicated, and I let it go with, "A gift."

Progressive Stadium used to be called The Jake and still should be. Jake is the name of my dog, a big bear dog with a gentle heart. I took him to a minor league game in Minnesota once. Dog night. He barked when the umpire made a bad call.

Our seats are behind third base in row X—X as in unknown, as in almost heaven. I follow Oscar up the steps, prepared to catch him if he teeters. We pass row M and Oscar takes a break, steps aside, sits in an empty seat while we let those climbing behind us pass. Oscar went through chemo and radiation, the whole nine yards, for non-Hodgkin's lymphoma, which we blame on Agent Orange and the weed killer Roundup. Chemo took the stuffing out of him. He tires quickly, gets out of breath. He droops. I want to ask if he's okay, but I don't want to pry, not here at the game surrounded by eavesdroppers. I sit in the empty seat behind him and take it all in, the green grass, the tan dirt of the pitcher's mound, the snow-white lines running from home plate into left and right field, the aroma of popcorn and hotdogs.

A woman coming up the steps eyes his seat.

"Just resting," Oscar says.

She smiles. "Take your time." Women love Oscar's boyish grin and his Grateful Dead T-shirt.

We climb higher, past row Q. Oscar slows. He grabs the back of empty seats and pulls himself up another step. We pass row T. Our seats are so high and the steps so steep, Sherpas work as vendors, carrying hotdogs and beer to the upper levels. We arrive and Oscar sits next to a scowling teenage boy flipping jellybeans over his shoulder and out of the stadium, maybe killing people walking far below.

I give the kid a look, one his father should be giving.

"I hate jellybeans," he says.

"I like them," Oscar says.

The kid dumps a pile into Oscar's hand.

"Do you know how fast those jellybeans are going when they hit the ground?" I ask.

The kid doesn't answer but gives me a look that says he's curious. I may work maintenance, but I live with a scientist. Numbers, numbers, numbers, she says. Velocity equals acceleration multiplied by time, and, I'm just guessing here, the jellybeans fall for five seconds. I do the math. "Those jellybeans are going one hundred and nine miles per hour when they hit the ground," I say. "They could kill someone."

I think this will stop the jellybean throwing.

"Cool," the kid says, and a handful go over his shoulder and out of the stadium before beginning their long fall, a potential mass murder.

I look at the man I assume is his father. He's wearing khaki cargo shorts that reveal snow-white legs. His goatee is shaggy and wild. Only the equation for gravity on the front of his too tight, mustard stained t-shirt suggests he's a man of science. He shrugs, sips his beer. "You forgot air resistance," he says. "And they fall for less than three seconds." He smiles. "Where's Sloane and Dr. Bakhatara?"

The guy annoys me, letting his son launch those deadly jellybeans and referring to Sloane by her first name while giving Rocky the title. Sloane has a Ph.D. with a post doc in high energy cosmology. "Dr. Sloane Wallace and Rocky are working," I say.

If the guy catches my sarcasm, he doesn't show it. The others seated around us introduce themselves. They're from Pakistan, Korea, Germany, South Africa. It's like Oscar and I are sitting in the middle of the physics U.N. They ask what we teach. I tell them Oscar and I work on grounds maintenance.

The game begins. First three innings, a pitchers' duel.

Fifth inning, score tied two runs each, I go down to the refreshment area and grab hotdogs, beer and lemonade. When I get back the physicists are discussing words. The guy sitting next to me, Vikram, who teaches at Case, says physics doesn't have the words to accurately describe reality. "Particle or wave?" he says. "Electrons are neither and both. Do we have a word for that?"

I try to catch as much of the discussion as possible. I will ask Sloane when I get home if she thinks we have the words to describe the mysteries of the universe.

"We don't have the words for a lot of things," the guy sitting next to Oscar says. "That's okay as long as we have the numbers."

I'm surprised the others agree, and soon they're trying to find words for things for which there is no word. "How about the reflection of a rising full moon on water?" Jellybean's father asks. "There should be a word for that."

"Moonglade," Oscar says.

The other physicists turn to Oscar and mumble, "Moonglade?"

Then we're back watching the game and eating our hotdogs. Oscar and I pass the binoculars back and forth. It takes us so close to the game we can almost count the stitches on the ball.

The breeze coming off the lake fades and the humidity becomes a weight pressing down on us. Dark clouds building in the west hide the setting sun. The science couple sitting on my left don't like the looks of those clouds. "Cumulonimbus," he says, finding the word for a thundercloud. After much discussion, they pick up and head down the steps.

The Cleveland catcher comes to bat. He's shorter than I imagined, but he's a hitter. We stand and cheer, ask the baseball gods for a homerun. He waits, takes the first five pitches—three balls, two strikes—and then cracks the next one over the right field fence. Prayers granted.

During the seventh inning stretch, Cleveland up 3–2, Oscar asks if Sloane gave me the binoculars.

"No," I say. "They were a gift from a girl who broke my previous pair when she used them to conk a bully over the head at a high school birthday party. Three years later these came in the mail." I hold up the binoculars. I shrug as if that's all there is to the story although I often think about this girl and how we sat on a bed-size boulder, our shoulders pressed together as we watched the comet Hale-Bopp, which might be a strange thing to be thinking about during a baseball game, especially one so close. I don't mention her name, the girl who gave me the binoculars. Her name was Cass, is Cass. She's no girl now. She's thirty-seven, a woman, an artist. I think about her and forget to sit down when the game starts again although it's not like I'm blocking anyone's view. Last I heard she lived in sunny California.

I remain standing throughout the inning. The premonition, the one that keeps running through my mind, the music and hand clapping, comes back again, comes in clearer, maybe because we're high up my premonition reception is better. It's like the curtains are about to open and someone special will step on stage although it's not yet clear who that might be. These gifts from the future start like the fragments of a dream, mostly emotion or maybe a fuzzy image, a bit of music. With time, however, the picture comes into focus. I think that's what it was like for Jocelyn Bell Burnell, a grad student looking for quasars. She helped build a radio telescope and later noticed a tiny bit of radio fuzz on the readouts. That first bit of fuzz was like a premonition, a hint of things to come. She looked over hundreds of pages of data every day and discovered those strange signals, almost invisible in all the radio noise, repeated. She studied them, did the math, and squeezed out all possible explanations until the solution came into focus: spinning neutron stars. She discovered pulsars.

"She should have gotten the Nobel Prize," I say.

I get strange looks from the U.N. of scientists, but no one asks who I'm talking about, which is okay with me because I'm just thinking out loud.

The Yankees—how we Cleveland fans hate the Yankees—come up to bat. Last inning. This is the game. Three outs and we win.

The Jumbotron shows the gate to the bullpen opening. The drama! The ace Cleveland closer is coming in while music blares over the speakers. There's hand clapping and Johnny Cash singing "God's Gonna Cut You Down." I tap Oscar on the shoulder. "You believe it? That song's been running through my head all day."

Oscar's clapping his hands with the music and paying no attention to me. I raise the binoculars to watch the ace closer step out from the bullpen and strut toward the mound, but you know how it is when you look through powerful binoculars, and you can't find what you're looking for. I mean, you might try to see a bird, but you can't find it, so you aim the binoculars up and down and sideways trying to locate the particular limb the bird is sitting on. That's what I'm doing. I see centerfield, the fence, the bleachers behind the bullpen. And then I spot a woman with binoculars looking back at me. I don't know if she's looking directly at me or just in my direction. Too far away to tell. I wave.

She waves.

This, I think, is pretty funny, the way our binocular gazing has us looking at each other at the same time. It's like two search lights beams locking onto each other. Then she lowers her binoculars.

I press my binoculars against my eyes and fiddle with the focus knob. I lean forward for a better look. The wide smile, the big eyes, the dimples. Not possible. I'm hallucinating. Maybe the heat or humidity or hotdogs have clouded my thinking, my vision. I can't hold the binoculars steady enough. They bounce around. I take a deep breath, slowly exhale, look again. Her black hair is short, cut like she's ready for a run, a yoga workout, a swim. She nods. It's her. It's Cass, the Cass I was just thinking about. I lower my binoculars and wave.

She waves.

The crowd cheers like they're happy for us, but the cheer is for the ace closer who has thrown two pitches for strikes. Cass holds up her hand. Two fingers and then an okay sign. I nod and give her a big okay sign back. Meet at gate two.

I'm momentarily thrown off balance. All I see is red. I lower the binoculars. The guy sitting to the right of Oscar is standing on the steps, getting ready to rush from the stadium, and his red hat is blocking my view. I lean sideways, see her again, and wave.

"That's two outs," Oscar says. Everyone in the stadium is standing, stomping their feet.

Cass holds up one finger. I nod. One more out. The man standing next to her watches the game, puts his fingers in his mouth and whistles. (I can't hear him, of course.) He's not paying any attention to her pointing her binoculars at row X and may not be husband, friend, or significant other.

The ace closer shrugs his shoulders, scowls at the batter. He owns the place. I focus on Cass. She smiles, acts like she's going to swing the binoculars. She makes hand signals and holds up a sketchpad on which she's written something. I feel like I'm back in the Federal building for my pre-induction physical and the doc's asking me to read the bottom line. I can't read it! I wave.

The crowd roars. Three outs! Game over. Cleveland wins. Fireworks!

Lightning flashes in the distance. The crowd oohs as I begin to count. One Mississippi, two Mississippi, three . . . I get to fourteen and thunder cracks. Another collective "Ooh" goes up from the crowd.

"About three miles away," I say to anyone listening. Being in the top row,

I'm afraid of becoming a human lightning rod. A voice over the loudspeaker urges everyone to proceed calmly toward an exit. I try to be calm, but I want to find Cass, and everyone is blocking the way. Oscar and I follow the jellybean and his dad. A wrong step, a slip on a discarded catsup-covered napkin, a hard bump from someone hurrying down the steps, and we're ass over teakettle. I worry about Oscar making it down safely, and I worry I might not get to the exit where Cass indicated we should meet, which I think is gate two although I'm not sure where that gate is. There are so many.

The players run off the field and into the dugouts. Oscar's moving pretty good, holding onto the railing. We're floating along in the crowd with no control over what direction we go. We get down to the next deck and are squeezed inside the stadium. We can barely move. We shuffle along. We get separated, jostled, bounced around. I'm afraid Oscar's going to get knocked down although there's no room to fall.

I can't leave him, and we'll never get through this crowd to another exit, so I make a quick decision. "Let's go," I say, taking him by the elbow as we emerge from the stadium. If I can get him to the truck quickly enough, I'll run back and try to catch Cass.

Four blocks. We parked four blocks from the stadium, and it takes me a few seconds to get oriented. As a cop waves us across an intersection it begins to rain. By the time we've crossed the street the rain is coming down in waves. I want to tell Oscar my plan, that I'm returning to the stadium once I get him in the truck, but the rain is coming down so hard and making so much noise he'll never hear me. Oscar speeds up the pace and I'm grateful.

We find the parking lot, the truck, and I open the door for Oscar and hand him the keys. "Be back," I say. "Lock the doors. I saw the binocular woman and . . .

"Go," he says.

I run. People are heading to their cars, and I'm dodging past them, weaving around groups intent on blocking my path. I get dirty looks as I splash through puddles and rivers of water, and, although I can see over most of the heads in front of me, I can't get around the bodies. Lightning flashes. Thunder booms and echoes off the downtown buildings. I feel like I'm running through the bottom of a canyon.

There is no gate two! The gates are identified by letters.

She held up two fingers. Maybe she was confused. I go to gate B, thinking that's the second gate. I yell her name. "Cass! Cass!"

No one answers. No one is there. The crowds are gone. Evaporated. Disappeared. I don't see anyone, not even maintenance people or security. For a moment I think I've gone to the wrong stadium or that I've time traveled back to another night when no game was played. I pace back and forth, calling her name.

"So, you didn't find her, this friend of yours?" Oscar asks when I return soaking wet to the truck. What he's really asking for is more information. Who is she? Why is she so important I ran four blocks through pouring rain to do what? Say hi?

"She signaled," I say. "She held up two fingers and then made an okay sign. I thought she was asking me to meet her at gate two, but there is no gate two."

"The gates go by letters," Oscar says.

"Yeah, I know that now."

"Maybe she was giving you her phone number. Any other numbers you remember?"

Shit. I bet he's right, but I don't remember any numbers other than two. Maybe a one. "We have history," I say.

Oscar waits. We're going thirty-five on a highway that has a speed limit twice that. I go any faster the tires are going to hydroplane. I decide to give him an example. "We were best friends in seventh grade for a few weeks one summer while she was visiting her grandparents.

"That's it? You knew her in seventh grade, and she gave you those binoculars?"

"No. I knew her for a few weeks during the summer *after* seventh grade. Then she had to get back with her parents. Father was military." Conversations like this, once started, are difficult to stop. I tell him about seeing her again at a party years later when we were in high school. "She was visiting a cousin," I say.

"The party where she whacked the guy in the head with my binoculars. We were watching the comet Hale-Bopp."

I look across the seat again, just checking to see if Oscar is following along, if he's still alive.

"A night with a lot of sparks?" he says.

"You could say that."

"A lot of sparks," he says.

A semi passes and the wash from the truck covers the windshield. I can't see the road. I can't see anything. I hug the steering wheel, but it does no good. I slow down even more, and eventually the truck is far enough ahead I can see its taillights and that we're still on the road.

Oscar says something, but the rain is hitting the roof of the cab so hard it's impossible to hear. I've been lost in a daydream and don't know if he's talking to me or himself. He talks to himself a lot.

I should steer the conversation back to the ballgame or the rain beating against the windows, but deep down I want to share more of our story. "You want to hear more?"

Oscar rubs his hands together. "Sure, this is getting good."

"Sloane and I were canoeing in the Boundary Waters last summer. Middle of nowhere. Just trees, water, moose, and bears. Then, up ahead, two women in a canoe were paddling toward us. Both wearing big floppy hats and topless. I didn't stare as we approached, not with Sloane sitting in front of me. Wouldn't have been respectful. I waved and said hello and kept paddling, very nonchalant, like I didn't notice the bare breasts. The two topless women called out hello and then the one called my name. 'Russ!' she said. I took a better look this time, and it was Cass, her hands quickly covering her breasts."

"Two canoes pass in the night," Oscar says.

"Or afternoon, something like that."

Oscar smacks his lips a few times, leans forward in his seat. "Not good to ignore fate. You ever think about giving her a call? Wouldn't that be something," he says.

"It would be something," I say. "But I'm with Sloane, sort of, and Cass and I, we're friends from childhood. I mean . . . I figured if I called, things might work out and we'd meet somewhere, go out to eat or catch a movie, maybe a romantic comedy, the kind where two characters meant for each other never seem to be able to get together. A date. Then one date would lead to another. There'd be handholding and one thing might lead to another if you know what I mean."

"Hell yes, I know what you mean. That's the point, one thing leading to another."

I drop Oscar off at his house and then do the three blocks home. I pull in the drive, kill the engine. The house is dark, no porchlight, no light in any of the windows. For a second I think the power must be out, but I see lights on at my neighbor's and across the street. Jake alone in a dark house. I wonder where Sloane is.

I'll go inside and hug that big bear dog. I'll get ice cream out of the freezer, give him a scoop, and then give myself two. But for a few minutes I'll sit in the truck and think about the way Cass and I orbit each other, never knowing when or where our next near miss will occur. Maybe we have our own fine-tuning problem. I'll try to discover the numbers, do the math, so I can understand the meaning of all that did and did not happen—and all that still, someday, could.

Roger Hart is a former science teacher and adjunct instructor at several colleges and universities. He has an MFA in creative writing from Minnesota State-Mankato and has had stories and essays published in more than thirty journals and magazines, including *Runner's World, Philadelphia Stories, The Sun,* and *Tampa Review.* He has won the *Ohio Writer* fiction contest, the *Third Coast* fiction contest, and the Marguerite McGlinn fiction contest. His story collection, *Erratics,* won the George Garrett Fiction Prize and was published by the Texas Review Press. His work has also been included in multiple anthologies, and his story "My Stuff" was selected for a dramatic reading at the Cleveland Playhouse. The first chapter of his novel, *Feather and Sel,* has been selected for publication by Leon Literary Review. He is the recipient of two grants from the Ohio Arts Council. He lives with his wife and two very large dogs in northern Montana where he is working on a new novel.

Some of these stories first appeared in the following magazines and anthologies:

The Boom Project: "The Bridge"
Coneflower Café: "Dew Drop Inn Diner"
Main Street Rag: "Anticipation"
Muddy Backroads: "Area 52"
Philadelphia Stories "Mysteries of the Universe"
Tampa Review: "Like Flying"
Texas Review: "How Coal Was Formed"
Third Coast: "Fireflies"

"Fireflies" won the *Third Coast* Fiction Contest
"Mysteries of the Universe" won the McGlinn Fiction Contest